CRYPTID NATION

CRYPTID ZOO BOOK 5

GERRY GRIFFITHS

SEVERED PRESS
HOBART TASMANIA

CRYPTID NATION

ISBN: 978-1-922323-49-1

ALSO BY GERRY GRIFFITHS

DEDICATION

This one is for you, Genene

1

COCKTAIL PARTY

FBI Special Agent Mark Jennings studied the faces around him, wondering if anyone could possibly be a threat to tonight's host. He stood rigid in the corner of the lavish room, watching the elegantly dressed guests mingle with drinks in hand, the constant drone of their voices interrupted occasionally by sudden bursts of laughter.

He checked his watch, realizing he was spread thin being the only agent at the event, wishing the rest of his team would hurry up and arrive, knowing they were stuck in the early evening D.C. gridlock.

Jennings had personally reviewed the guest list, each person subjected to a thorough background check in the Bureau's database, all one hundred and ten attending Senator Jonathan Rollins's cocktail party including the catering staff.

He rested a little easier when the two members of his team showed up and were escorted into the main room by the Rollins's new housekeeper, Eva.

"Welcome to the party," Jennings said to Special Agent Anna Rivers, dressed in a tailored black pants suit.

"Sorry, Mark, we got—"

"I know, you don't have to apologize," Jennings said.

"So where do you want us?" Special Agent Mack Hunter asked, placing his hands on his hips, his unbuttoned jacket revealing the butt of his service pistol visible in his shoulder holster.

"Anna, patrol the upstairs," Jennings said. "Mack, take over here. Keep an eye on the senator. He's over by the fireplace. I'm going to the kitchen to check on Mrs. Rollins."

"Sure thing," Mack said. He stepped into the throng of guests and wove his way over to the closed French doors of the balcony overlooking the glittering lights of the Washington D.C. area with its iconic landmarks.

Jennings found Margo Rollins in the breakfast nook just off the kitchen, out of the way of the steady foot traffic of servers carrying trays filled with flutes of expensive imported champagne and platters of bite-size hors d'oeuvres.

"Quite the event," Jennings said. He stood at the edge of the threshold so as not to impose on Mrs. Rollins's personal space.

"To be honest, I'll be so glad when the night's over," Mrs. Rollins replied. She held a large wineglass and took a gulp. "Any progress on finding the person responsible for sending those death threats to my husband?"

"All we know at this point is that someone is trying to scare him into stepping down as chairman of the committee overseeing the U.S Fish and Wildlife Service as he's made it clear that he plans to vote down this proposed Endangered Species bill. Rest assured, we do have some leads."

"What imbecile would even think of passing such legislature to protect these creatures? My God, they're everywhere. Surely they've seen the senseless attacks on the news?" Mrs. Rollins finished her glass and poured herself some more wine from a bottle on the table. "My husband tells me you were lead investigator at Cryptid Zoo."

"That's right."

"Was it as bad as what happened at Carter Wilde's high-rise?"

"Yes, ma'am," Jennings said. "Hard to believe that was nearly a year and a half ago."

"And it's only gotten worse," Mrs. Rollins said, shaking her head.

Jennings cocked his head and put his finger to the miniature transmitter tucked in his ear and heard, "Mark, this is Anna."

"If you'll excuse me," Jennings said to Mrs. Rollins and stepped away. "What is it?" he said into the tiny speaker attached to the cuff of his jacket.

"I think I heard a scream."

"Hold your position, I'll be right there." Jennings entered the main room filled with important politicians and their spouses gathered in small groups.

He glanced over at the French doors. Mack wasn't there. He spotted him standing near the foyer by the front entrance. The agent acknowledged Jennings with a wave that he had overheard Anna's transmission.

Jennings proceeded warily up the wide staircase curving up to the second floor, his left hand gliding up the smoothly polished railing of the teak banister, his right hand inside his jacket, resting on the handgrip of his service pistol holstered on his hip.

As he gradually went up the stairs, the noise level on the ground floor dissipated slowly so by the time he made it to the landing and was a short distance down the hall, the revelry down below had softened to a dull roar.

He spoke into his speaker cuff. "Anna, I'm upstairs. Where are you?"

"Down the hall and to the right. I'm outside the door where I heard the scream."

"Stay put." Jennings heard a high-pitched wail and raced toward the bend.

"I'm going in," Anna said into his ear.

Jennings ran around the corner and spotted Anna stepping into the room.

Reaching the doorway, he immediately felt a gust of wind. Across the dark bedroom the curtains billowed in the night breeze, the window glass smashed from the frame, shards glinting on the carpet in the moonlight.

Anna stood by the bed. A young girl sat with her back to the headboard, clutching the comforter to her chin.

Jennings made a quick sweep. "Amy, is it still in your room?" he asked the senator's nine-year-old daughter.

"I don't know," Amy whimpered.

"It's okay, honey." Anna put a knee on the bed to be close to the child and kept her attention on the gloomy room. She glanced over at Jennings. "Think it flew back out?"

Jennings stared at the open door to the walk-in closet.

It was pitch black inside.

He could hear leathery wings rustling together like dried leaves on a tree in an autumn breeze. "Get Amy off the bed. Nice and slow," Jennings whispered, training his gun on the closet doorway. He took out his tactical flashlight and held it against the gun barrel and advanced toward the noise inside the closet.

Jennings flicked on the flashlight.

The beam caught the creature square in the face. It looked like a giant fox with vicious teeth. The Ahool stood five feet tall with its wings tucked close behind its furry body. It recoiled from the bright light and hissed, then sprang forward in an attempt to gain flight.

Jennings shot the megabat twice, striking it in the head and dead center in the chest. The creature sailed out of the closet and did a nosedive onto the carpet.

"That's strange," Anna said looking down at the dead creature. "They usually don't come out at night."

3

"You're right. Megbats are too big to have echolocation. They usually hunt during the day." Jennings stepped toward the busted out window. A full moon hung high in the night sky like a calling card over the brightly lit city.

Suddenly there was a disturbance downstairs with glass shattering and guests screaming.

"What the hell?" Anna said, shooting a glance at Jennings.

Jennings spoke into his speaker cuff. "Mack, what's going on?"

"We're being attacked by megabats."

"Tell everyone not to run and get to the floor," Jennings said, hearing the bedlam in his earpiece.

"Easier said than done. It's pure panic down here."

"Then do something to get everyone's attention."

Jennings turned to Anna. "The breaker box is in the master bedroom closet," he said, moving toward the door. "Take Amy with you and kill the lights downstairs."

Anna grabbed Amy by the hand and they rushed out into the hall.

Jennings heard a single gunshot from downstairs.

A few seconds later, Mack's voice sounded in Jennings's ear. "We've lost the lights."

"That was Anna," Jennings said. "Tell everyone to stay on the floor. These damn things can't see shit in the dark." Jennings shined his light and bolted down the hall.

He reached the top of the stairs and panned the beam down below.

People were lying flat on their bellies or huddled behind furniture.

Jennings counted five megabats staggering blindly in the darkened room.

A man let out a scream.

Jennings raced down the stairs.

Another flashlight came on: Mack's. He directed his torch on the megabat straddling the screaming man. The creature dug its talons into the man's chest, lowered its head, and bit the top of his skull.

Mack fired once. The megabat screeched when the bullet ripped through its neck causing it to slump onto the floor.

The creatures made strange chattering noises as if their teeth hurt then together bellowed a loud trill-like screech forcing the guests to cover their ears.

An Ahool felt about the floor with its sharp-clawed feet and stepped on a prone woman, who immediately screamed. The giant bat dug its talons into the back of her dress and into her flesh, spread open its wings, and flapped upward, hoisting the hysterical woman off of the floor.

Mack shined his flashlight on the creature and shot it in the head. Bloody fur splattered onto an oil painting hanging on the wall of George Washington standing regally in a Durham boat amongst oarsmen crossing the icy Delaware River.

The megabat crashed to the floor on top of the woman.

Jennings marched into the room and shot a creature about to jump down off a couch.

The remaining Ahools took flight through the damaged French doors from which they had broken through and gained entrance. Jennings watched the megabats fly into the night, joining up with a flock heading away from the city.

"Anna, turn the lights back on," Jennings said into his speaker cuff.

A second later the room was bright again, people sprawled on the floor looking disoriented and disheveled, some of the women crying.

Jennings immediately went over to Senator Rollins who was picking himself up off the floor. "Are you hurt, sir?" Jennings asked.

"No, I'm fine." The senator gave Mack a tolerant look. A time back, Rollins had been campaigning in the presidential race when his oldest daughter, Caroline, who was now away at college, had been kidnapped. After her rescue, Mack had made a comment that Rollins had used for his platform, which resulted in so much negative press the senator was forced to withdraw from the race. A bitter pill to swallow as the agent had saved his daughter from a diabolical killer. "We need to get these people some help."

"I already made the call," Mack said.

"Good," Senator Rollins said. "Damn Ahools."

"One got into your daughter's bedroom but we killed it," Jennings said. "You needn't worry, she's fine. I have an agent with her now."

"What's the current threat level on those things; a 2?" the senator asked.

"The Cryptid Warning System bumped them to a Level-3."

"This keeps up they'll be at the top of the chart."

"Let's hope not," Jennings said, wishing he had never heard of a damn cryptid.

2

MORNING JOE

Jack Tremens stepped onto his porch and looked out at the rolling hills of grassland and majestic oak trees bordered by the dense forest of junipers and ponderosa pines. He could see the church steeple and the town rooftops of Rocklin Falls five miles away down in the valley. He stayed clear of the busted-down railing, sipping his coffee, and turned slowly when the screen door opened behind him.

"They're not here yet?" Professor Nora Howard asked as she came out to join Jack.

"Miguel had to make a stop on the way," Jack replied. He held out his mug so Nora could take a drink. "So what are your plans?"

"Go into town. Sheriff Stone has some updates for me. There have been more sightings."

"Where do these things keep coming from?" Jack asked.

"I wish I knew."

"Surely they can't be breeding that fast."

"It does happen this time of year but I think something else has caused their numbers to increase."

"What, short of making new ones?"

Nora gave Jack a strange look.

"You're not seriously suggesting..."

"I think McCabe is at it again."

"You're saying he's out there somewhere creating these creatures and setting them loose?"

"That's right," Nora said.

Jack knew better than to question Nora's judgment. She was the cryptozoologist and geneticist that had co-created the unique creatures at the Cryptid Zoo facility along with Dr. Joel McCabe, who had later sabotaged the project, and after being sent to prison, had escaped and gone into hiding.

"But why? And where would he get the money to set up a new lab?"

"I don't know. Maybe somehow he got back in Carter Wilde's good graces," Nora said, handing Jack's mug back.

"That's insane. McCabe tried to ruin Wilde."

"I know it doesn't make sense but you never know. The two are so twisted. Wilde is so obsessed with cryptids, he might be crazy enough to fund McCabe. It's almost as if they have this symbiotic relationship. One feeding off the other."

"That would certainly explain the influx of cryptids," Jack said. He turned to the sound of an engine approaching and saw Miguel's Ford F-150 coming up the gravel driveway with a load of lumber and building material stacked in the long bed.

"I can't believe it," Nora said. "You guys are going to work on the barn?"

"Told you we would. Best to reinforce those beams before Lennie knocks the place down."

"He can't help it if he's a clumsy oaf."

"Yeah, well, do me a favor and don't invite him onto the porch again."

"Poor thing," Nora said with a smile. "He only leaned on it. You should have seen the surprised look on his face when the railing collapsed."

"I bet it was really comical. Too bad you didn't post it."

"Jack! Be nice."

"You're not the one having to follow him around fixing things."

"You wouldn't say that if he was your son."

"If he was, we'd be the talk of the town."

Miguel Walla got out of the passenger side of the truck and waved to Jack and Nora. "Hey, guys." His wife, Maria, was sitting behind the steering wheel and acknowledged the couple on the porch. The Walla's black Labrador, Rosie, jumped out of the cab and romped about the yard.

"I'll be right there," Jack hollered.

"Take your time." Miguel went to the rear of the truck and ripped off the red rag stapled to the end of the longest post extending over the tailgate.

"Promise you two will be careful," Jack said to Nora as she started for the steps.

"Jack, quit your worrying. We'll be fine." Nora lifted the bottom of her jacket to reveal the small handgun holstered on her belt since it had been deemed legal to carry a firearm for protection against cryptids.

"Should we invite Miguel and Maria for dinner?" Jack asked.

"Why, are you cooking?"

7

"No. I thought you could pick something up after you get Sophia from school."

"Sure, we could do that."

"Great. I better get down there and help Miguel offload so you guys can have the truck."

"You should let Lennie help," Nora said.

"Not on your life," Jack replied and raced down the steps.

3

LATEST UPDATES

Nora spotted a car leaving a parking spot in front of the sheriff's office and motioned to Maria who turned in.

"How's that for service," Maria said, shutting off the truck.

"Coming in?" Nora asked. "I shouldn't be any longer than thirty minutes."

"That's okay. It'll give me time to run some errands. I'll meet you back here and we can grab brunch at the cafe before school let's out."

"Oh, that's right. Sophia has minimum day."

Maria waited until Nora got out then climbed down and locked up the truck. "See you in a bit," she said and headed off down the sidewalk.

Nora pushed through the glass front door and went inside the sheriff's office.

Sheriff Abraham "Abe" Stone stood behind the counter with a cup of coffee. He smiled at Nora and said, "Care for some? It's not that great but it's hot."

"I'm okay, thanks though." Nora spotted a black garbage bag on a tabletop next to the fax machine. "What do you have there?"

"Something I want you to see."

Nora watched Abe slip on plastic gloves. She grabbed a pair out of the box on the desk and put them on while Abe held the bottom of the trash bag and raised it up so the object inside slipped out.

"Is that one of Clare's goats?" she asked, knowing that Abe's wife ran a business hiring out her flock for manicuring farmland.

"It was."

Nora leaned over the dead animal. It was as thin as a tapestry. "What happened? Did it get run over?"

"No. We found it in one of the pens with its guts splattered everywhere."

"And that was when, a few days ago?"

"No, Clare said it was alive before we went to bed last night. She always goes out with Rounder and checks the goats before we turn in."

"But it's just hide and bone."

"Listen to this." Abe picked up the carcass by the neck and hindquarters and gave it a shake. The bones inside rattled like gravel in a bag. "Every bone in its body was shattered."

The fax machine turned on loudly.

A CWS dispatch with photos of the latest cryptid sightings fed out onto the tray. A score of pictures printed before the fax machine shut off.

The sheriff placed the dead goat back in the trash bag and stepped over to the fax machine. He stripped off his gloves and picked up the pile of pages from the tray. He leafed through the photos slowly. Once he was through looking at a few, he handed those to Nora.

She'd seen similar pictures before. Many of them taken by frightened people on their cell phones or images captured on outdoor security cameras.

Nora studied each photo.

A small troop of Bigfoot skulked through a forest.

Giant Thunderbirds glided on a thermal lift; the picture taken from the window of a commercial passenger plane.

Outdoor surveillance shot of an Mgnwa, tall as the horses the huge, black panther had cornered in a corral.

Menacing flocks of Ahools flying over a field.

A pack of bloodsucking Chupacabras hunched over a dead pastoral animal.

An enormous Bergman's bear safely caught on camera with a long telephoto lens.

Two aerial pictures taken from a helicopter: one showing cars plummeting into a sinkhole, the other of a Mongolian death worm undermining and demolishing a freeway.

Abe handed Nora the last few pictures without looking at them. "Welcome to the new normal."

4

BARN RAZING

Jack knew when they had bought the place six months ago it would need some work but Nora loved the view and it was ideal having a barn behind the ranch-style home. He had to admit it was nice sitting out on the porch during the evenings, gazing at the stars and the glittering town lights in the valley below.

Since they had moved in, Miguel had helped Jack with remodeling the outdated kitchen and putting in new bathroom fixtures. Together, they had painted the house inside and out. Even tearing out the old deck and building a new one with stairs, including the wraparound railing that was now in need of repair thanks to Lennie.

Lennie sensed Jack was upset with him—even though Jack would never berate the big lummox—and had gone off to forage in the forest, which wasn't unusual because that is where Lennie spent most of his time anyway when he wasn't on the property.

Jack went over to the stack of lumber piled outside the barn door and picked up a four-by-four post. He carried it over his shoulder inside the barn. Miguel was up in the loft, nailing down fresh floorboards.

"Almost done up there?" Jack asked, laying the post on the ground.

"Yeah, last one," Miguel called down, firing off his nail gun.

"Good, then we can switch out this rotted post." Jack walked over to his workbench and sorted through a box of metal braces until he found the right size. Even though he didn't have the skill-set of a journeyman carpenter like Miguel, he liked to work with wood and felt he had become an adequate do-it-yourselfer. He had even amassed a decent amount of hand and power tools, tackling various projects.

He had no idea what the previous owners had intended for the barn, though there were a few separate stalls that suggested it might have been used for sheltering small livestock like sheep at one time. The interior was big enough to easily park seven or eight vehicles inside. Nora's plan was to subdivide the space into living quarters for Lennie and a work area for Jack, which was what they were trying to currently accomplish.

While Jack waited for Miguel to come down from the loft, he decided to go over and give Rosie some attention. She was lying on a pile of straw a few feet away from the open barn doors, watching the entrance. She glanced up at Jack for a split second when he knelt beside her then returned her gaze to the outside where she could see the piled wood and a corner of the house.

"Anything out there, girl?" Jack said, ruffling her scruff.

Rosie answered with a soft moan.

"Hey, you want to grab this?" Miguel said, halfway down the ladder. He held out the heavy nail gun. Jack stood, went over, and grabbed the tool. Miguel climbed the rest of the way down.

"Want to break for lunch? There's some fried chicken in the fridge," Jack said, putting the nail gun on the workbench.

"From town or did Nora make it?" Miguel asked.

"Aren't you the picky one."

"Sorry, I just don't care for—"

Rosie started to growl.

Jack and Miguel turned and saw the dog rise quickly to her feet.

"There's something out there," Miguel whispered.

Besides wearing their tool belts, they also had holstered sidearms on their opposite hips. Jack, a Colt.44 Magnum revolver; Miguel, his .357 Desert Eagle semi-automatic pistol. Both men stood ready but didn't draw their guns.

Jack heard heavy footfalls outside coming toward the barn's front entrance. "Get ready," he told Miguel.

Rosie stepped back and began barking.

"Here we go," Miguel said.

Two giant bears lumbered in on all fours through the open doorway. They stood shoulder to shoulder, blocking out much of the sun. Each animal huffed and made guttural noises that resonated within the barn walls. They had coarse wiry hair, big heads, and thick massive legs with huge sharp-clawed paws.

"Looks like we got ourselves a couple of Bergman's bears," Miguel said matter-of-factly like they were as common a sight as spotting two deer in the woods.

"You better call back Rosie before she gets hurt."

Miguel stepped toward the ladder and called out in a low but stern voice, "Rosie, come here!"

Rosie's hackles were up, shoulders bunched, ready for a fight.

Jack knew the sixty-pound dog would be no match against the two bears. He figured each one had to weigh at least 700 pounds.

Rosie must have realized the odds weren't in her favor because she began to retreat a step at a time back toward Miguel, never once taking her eyes off the two massive beasts.

The bear standing twenty feet away in front of Jack rose up onto its hind legs. It stood over eight feet tall. The other bear stood up as well. They took in deep breaths and roared, the sudden boom scaring off a row of starlings perched on the loft windowsill up above.

The bears raised their front paws and stomped deeper into the barn.

"We might not have a choice here," Miguel said, reaching for his pistol.

Jack had a better idea. He saw the post on the ground and picked it up near the middle, as it was heavy.

"What are you doing?" Miguel asked.

"I'm about to go medieval on these things." Jack held the post like a jousting knight would a lance and ran at the closest bear. The end of the post struck the bear in the lower belly. It was enough to get the animal to grunt and back up; but only for a moment. It began to advance and Jack hit it again.

The bear did a downward swipe with its front paw and split the post in half.

"Jesus," Jack said, and stepped back.

The bear nearest to Miguel dropped down on all fours and charged.

Miguel ducked behind the ladder while Rosie bolted into a stall.

With its head down, the bear crashed into the rotted post the men had planned to replace which turned out to be supporting a load-bearing beam because the loft flooring above came crashing down all around them with falling planks and raining straw.

The bear rose out of the debris before the dust could settle and shook off.

Jack and Miguel backed toward the stall where Rosie stood, bearing her fangs.

Both bears began to move in.

The men had no choice but to draw their weapons.

A huge shape charged into the barn and rushed the bears.

Jack was relieved to see Lennie.

The twelve-foot tall Yeren always reminded Jack of an elongated orangutan with its thick reddish-brown hair and its black leathery face and chest. Lennie's arms were as long as Jack was tall. He hadn't taken Lennie to the feed store lately where they had a scale equipped to handle the heavy stuff but he figured the Chinese Bigfoot weighed well over a thousand pounds, especially the way he could pack it away, consuming a hundred pounds of food in a single sitting.

Lennie grabbed a bear by the hind leg and pulled it off its feet.

He spun the bear around, smashing it into the barn wall, creating a ragged, gaping hole as the animal flew out and landed on the dirt.

Lennie turned and marched up to the other bear, and with one powerful punch, struck the animal squarely in the snout.

The bear whimpered and lumbered out through the open barn doors.

"What took you so long?" Jack asked Lennie, Nora's pet cryptid that she had personally created at the bioengineering laboratory while employed at Cryptid Zoo.

Lennie hung his head and kicked some boards on the ground with his big toes.

Jack looked around at all the damage then patted Lennie on the forearm. "It's okay, big guy. This wasn't entirely your fault."

Lennie looked down at Jack and blew him a wet raspberry.

"Thanks," Jack said, wiping his face with the back of his hand.

"Well, I guess this time we were lucky," Miguel said, taking a knee to hug Rosie.

Bergman's bears were the number one threat according to the CWS, the largest one ever recorded measuring 16 feet tall and weighing 4000 pounds.

Jack smiled at Miguel. "Let's hope the mother doesn't show up looking for her cubs."

5

LOCKDOWN

After grabbing a quick meal at the Rocklin Falls Cafe, Nora and Maria headed over to pick Maria's daughter, Sophia up from elementary school. Many of the parents had already showed up with their vehicles so Maria had to park the truck halfway down the block from the school. Nora got out and waited on the sidewalk for Maria. The bell sounded signaling the end of the school day.

A harried woman gave Nora a quick smile as she scurried by to go pick up her child. Nora saw more parents standing at the pickup area, waiting for the children to come out of the main entrance in single file with their classmates and teachers.

Nora and Maria walked through the parking lot reserved for the school staff and stepped up on the sidewalk to wait with the other parents.

"This must be such a hassle for working parents," Nora said. "Having to make special arrangements when their kids get out early."

"I've heard the complaints, believe me," Maria said. "Thankfully they only get out early once a week."

Nora noticed many of the people looked much older than parents with elementary-aged children. Keeping her voice low, she noted, "There seems to be a lot of grandparents here."

"Such is the cycle of life." Maria looked at Nora. "So, have you and Jack set a date?"

"Not yet."

"What are you waiting for? Christmas?" Maria quipped.

"No," Nora said and stifled a laugh. "I'm just nervous if we do and have our own kids, what kind of world would we be bringing them into?" She saw the front glass doors swing open as the first students began to file out.

"You shouldn't think that way," Maria assured her. "I mean, look at Sophia. She's adjusted perfectly—"

A high-pitched alarm sounded and kept blasting.

"What's that?" Nora said.

"Oh my God, that's the emergency alert. It's a school lockdown. I have to get in there and find Sophia." Maria dashed toward the open doors. Nora ran after her friend, and just managed to get inside before the doors automatically closed and locked.

Nora saw rows of students standing in the long hall.

"Everyone back to your classes," instructed a man wearing a suit and tie.

Nora recognized the school's principle. She shouted, "Mr. Calvin!" and hoped he could hear her over the clamoring children shuttling back to their classrooms.

The principle turned. "Professor Howard, what are you doing here?"

"I'm here with Maria Walla to pick up her daughter. What's going on?"

"One of the teachers called to say that there was a problem in the computer lab and to put the school on lockdown."

"What? The kids are still in the classroom?" Maria asked.

"I won't know until I get there."

"Where is the computer lab?" Nora asked.

"It's down the hall and toward the west wing. I'm headed that way now."

"Let me tag along."

"Sure."

Nora looked at Maria. "Coming?"

"Damn straight. Computer lab is Sophia's last class."

The three hurried down the hall as children funneled into the classrooms and the doors slammed shut.

Entering the west wing, Nora could hear children screaming farther down the corridor. Mr. Calvin reached the door to the computer room and was about to turn the knob when Nora grabbed him by the wrist having glanced through the small glass window and witnessing what was happening inside the classroom.

A large plate glass window was smashed out with jagged edges; leaving glass everywhere on the floor amongst upended desks and shattered computer monitors. A chair tumbled across the room in the direction of the twenty kids huddled against the far wall with their teacher.

"What's going on?" Maria asked, trying to glance through the small window on the classroom door.

Nora pressed her face against the glass. She couldn't see what was causing the commotion in the classroom. "I don't know but we have to get in there. You both ready?"

Maria and Mr. Calvin nodded.

Nora threw open the door and looked to her left.

A giant black bird squawked and beat its powerful wings, swiping computers from the few desks still standing. It had a wingspan of over eight feet wide and was knocking things over as it thrashed about, appearing to be in pain.

Mr. Calvin grabbed a fire extinguisher off the wall. He held it by the handle and pulled the pin. He looked at Nora and Maria. "I'll hold it off while you get everyone out."

"My God, it's a Thunderbird chick," Nora said.

"What the hell's wrong with it?" Maria asked, waving to the teacher instructing the children to stay close to the wall as they crept toward the open door. Sophia was near the end of the line.

The young bird crashed onto the floor, using its wings to push itself onto its feet.

Nora could tell it was sickly by the way it staggered and had trouble keeping its head erect.

Mr. Calvin aimed the nozzle of the fire extinguisher and hosed the giant bird with white foam. The fire retardant covered most of the bird's chest and parts of its wings.

Nora heard a humming sound.

A dark cloud of black flies the size of prunes flew out of the feathered body of the Thunderbird chick and swarmed the children.

"Everyone cover your faces!" Mr. Calvin yelled as the children screamed. He walked up and sprayed the flies, chasing them out through the opening in the window frame.

The Thunderbird chick collapsed on the floor.

Nora approached the cryptid, while Mr. Calvin ushered everyone out of the room.

Maria knelt to embrace Sophia as she ran into her arms. "You're safe now."

Mr. Calvin put the extinguisher on the floor and stood beside Nora. "It looks dead."

"It is."

"Don't tell me those flies killed it?"

Nora dropped to one knee to get a closer look at the bird. She saw movement in the chest. "Wait a minute. I think it's alive."

Suddenly, a white head popped out between the feathers. The wriggling thing looked like a wet plastic-gloved thumb.

"What the hell is that?" Mr. Calvin said.

Nora looked up at the principle. "I'm afraid we have a more serious problem."

6

BEING BRAVE

Nora stood in the hall, concluding her call with Sheriff Stone. She slipped her cell phone in her jacket pocket and returned to the room. Maria occupied the chair beside the hospital bed and was holding Sophia's hand. The girl wore a green hospital gown and sat on the edge of the thick mattress, kicking her feet nervously against the lowered handrail.

"How're you doing?" Nora asked Sophia.

"I'm scared."

"I know. It will all be over before you know it."

Maria looked up at Nora. "So what did the sheriff have to say?"

"They incinerated the diseased Thunderbird chick and fumigated the classroom."

"Thank God. The nurse informed me the doctor would be in shortly."

"Oh, good. Did she mention how the other children are doing?" Nora asked.

"Of the twenty kids, only seven were bitten," Maria said, and then glanced at her daughter. "Poor Sophia being the worst."

"Oh my."

Sophia looked at Nora. "Is it going to hurt?" The girl looked like she was about to cry.

"No honey, but I don't want you to get freaked out."

They heard a child scream from another room down the hall.

"Are you sure?"

"They're probably just scared, that's all. I promise, you won't feel a thing. When the doctor comes in, I'll be right here to talk you through it."

A minute later, Dr. Aaron Drake came into the room pushing a small cart with a metal pan of surgical tools, strips of gauze, and a bottle of disinfectant.

"Hello Sophia," Dr. Drake said.

"Hi," Sophia replied sheepishly.

The doctor looked at Nora and Maria. "If you don't care to watch, you might want to go down the hall to the waiting room. I can have someone get you when I'm finished."

"If it's okay, we'd like to stay," Nora said. Maria nodded that she wanted to remain in the room as well.

"Then let's get started. Mrs. Walla, if I could get you to switch places with Sophia, I'd like to use that chair," Dr. Drake said. While Sophia got down from the bed, the doctor grabbed another chair that was by the window and positioned it so that it was perpendicular to the other chair.

Sophia sat in a chair while Dr. Drake occupied the one facing her. He pulled the cart toward him so that he had easy access to the items on the top shelf.

"I'm going to ask you to lower your gown just a bit," the doctor said.

Sophia pulled the garment down enough to modestly cover her chest.

Nora and Maria leaned in for a closer look at the tiny bite marks covering Sophia's shoulders and upper arms.

"I'm going to start with the one on your left shoulder," Dr. Drake said and grabbed a pair of tweezers from the tray.

Sophia took one look at the intrusive tool and gasped, "Mom?"

Dr. Drake looked at Maria. "It's the best way, I assure you."

"Aren't you going to give her a shot to numb the pain?"

The doctor shook his head.

"There's no need," Nora said to Maria. "The flies already anesthetized the bite wounds just like mosquitoes do so you don't feel them sucking your blood."

"What, you're saying these flies are like mosquitoes?" Maria said.

"Actually, it's the other way around," Nora explained. "Mosquitoes are actually a species of fly."

"I didn't know that."

"Ladies, if we could begin," the doctor said, interrupting them politely.

"Oh, I'm sorry," Nora apologized. "Go ahead."

The doctor smiled at his patient. "It might be better if you look away, Sophia. I promise, you won't feel a thing."

Sophia turned her head and stared at the window.

Dr. Drake spread the tweezers tips apart slightly and stuck the points into Sophia's flesh. He probed the instrument deeper into the skin surface down into the epidermis. He leaned forward to further examine the wound. "Ah, I see it."

Sophia started to turn her head to watch what the doctor was doing.

"No, honey. Keep looking away," Maria said, her eyes growing wide as she watched the doctor begin to extract something white out of Sophia's shoulder. "My God, what is that?" she gasped, unable to contain herself.

"What Mama?" Sophia asked, still staring out the window.

"It's okay," Nora said. "It's almost out."

"What is?" Sophia turned just as the doctor pulled a long elastic maggot out of her flesh. As soon as it was completely out, the larva sprang back to its natural plumpness.

Dr. Drake held the squirming maggot over the metal pan and released it. "One down, four to go."

Sophia looked down and watched the maggot wriggling in a tiny blob of slime.

"How are you doing?" the doctor asked Sophia. "Do you need to take a break?"

"No, it didn't hurt."

"That's my brave girl," Maria said. She looked at Nora. "So what were those things again in the classroom?"

"Botflies. That maggot in the dish is actually an internal parasite. They live in a host until they mature into flies and can crawl out of the festered wounds."

Maria glanced at Sophia to make sure she wasn't frightened; instead, the young girl seemed intrigued.

Doctor Drake took that as a sign to continue and started to extract the next maggot from Sophia's upper arm.

"It's good that we decided to get the children medical attention right away," Nora said. "Normally it would take a week or so for the maggots to get this size."

"So what do you think is causing this to happen so fast?" Maria asked.

"You saw how big those flies were in the classroom."

"They were huge."

"Exactly. I think they got that way from feeding off the blood of the Thunderbird chick. It would explain its sickly condition and the maggots' rapid rate of growth."

Dr. Drake tossed another maggot into the tray. He looked up at Nora. "We better pray this doesn't become an infestation."

"What do you mean?" Maria asked.

"It means," Nora said, "Dr. McCabe has gotten sloppy. He's created cryptids with defective genes, which are susceptible to a wide range of diseases. Which will be catastrophic unless we can stop him."

7

BOTANIC-WONDER

Laney Moss walked from the cottage and took the short path through the trees to the greenhouse. As always, she knew better than to just waltz right in without giving Allen's bodyguards a moment to detect her scent. "Okay, boys. I'm coming in."

She could hear twisting wood groan just inside of the main doorway like the creaking hull of a frigate in high seas as the two twelve-foot tall man-eating trees resumed their normal sentry posts. She stepped through the entranceway and glanced up at the stone-still trees with their bough arms and long-fingered branches down by their sides; their treetop maws tightly closed.

The new 3,000 square foot building was a step-up from the previous structure that was made up of wood framework and glass panels and was purposely set on fire and burned to the ground over a year ago by arsonists. Thirty feet wide and 90 feet long, the newer model greenhouse was built with sturdy galvanized steel with double-pane tempered glass set in aluminum frames.

Normally such an operation would have stringent biosphere temperature stabilization and humidity hydrometers and a computer system that would analyze every horticultural requirement such as regulating time-set irrigation, identifying soil chemical deficiencies, and ensuring the proper nutrients were dispersed to ensure healthy and sustainable plant growth.

None of that was necessary as Laney's husband, Allen, had an unusually green thumb. Actually, he had more than that.

He was green all over.

Since his metamorphosis over three years ago, Allen's human molecular structure had swiftly changed from tissue, bone, and internal organs to metabolized cellulose, plastids, and cytoplasm, converting him into the botanic-wonder.

Horrified at first, Allen soon learned to deal with the life-altering experience thanks to Laney's undying support and love for her husband.

Not only did Allen prove to be a gifted gardener, he also possessed the ability to communicate telepathically with the plant world.

The one-of-a-kind horticulturist shared a mutualistic interaction with all living vegetation whether domestically grown or thriving out in the wilds. He often kidded Laney that he thought of himself as a family pet with a degree in veterinarian medicine that could empathize and talk with his patients.

It was Allen's compassion for others and his altruistic crusade to end global suffering that compelled him to work tirelessly each and every day.

Allen never ceased to amaze Laney. She gazed at the array of flourishing specimens, many listed in botany and environmental scientific journals, some created solely from Allen's vivid imagination.

Four rows of garden beds extended the length of the greenhouse. Allen devoted the two innermost rows of planters for growing his cure-all crops, along with plants grown to generate a steady income and be sold at the Moss's nursery located a short distance away on the property.

The surrounding beds were a defensive perimeter of deadly cryptid plants.

Even though Laney wore a hemp bracelet that gave off a pheromone and protected her against being attacked, she knew better to stay clear of the vampire vines clinging to the sides of the planters. If an unsuspecting person got too close, the fibrous, dark blue roots would latch out and grab hold, blistering the skin and immediately suck their blood.

Allen had positioned yate-veo trees about the greenhouse. The killer trees had dagger-like thorns capable of impaling a victim and draining the body entirely of blood.

Large blades of razor-sharp palmettos lined the outskirts of the planter boxes while strangler vines and creepers waited a trap in case of intruders.

Laney became aware of soothing classical music playing softly from hidden speakers positioned inside the greenhouse. The volume had been turned down so low that she hadn't detected it at first, the background noise more like an ominous breeze. She recognized the symphonic piece by Franz Listz: *Les Preludes,* which was one of her favorites. If she closed her eyes and listened, the imagery of a new dawning day always blossomed in her mind.

Often when Allen worked alone, he loved to crank up the volume to invigorate his plants as Laney could hear the music playing from the cottage.

Laney spotted Allen working with his hydrophytes, their long tentacle roots floating beneath the hydroponics water tank's surface. He was holding up a droopy-stemmed plant that had turned yellow.

She was glad to see Allen in his human form—even though he was green as a pea pod—as sometimes when she wasn't around he had a tendency to change shape and blend in with the surrounding foliage.

Normally, Allen preferred not to wear clothes. It was important his skin absorb natural sunlight through photosynthesis and convert the energy into sugar glucose to fuel his cells, as he no longer had the ability to eat human-style food.

"Looks like you have a sick patient," Laney said.

"It's got a bad case of chlorosis. I'm going to have to adjust the nitrate levels." Allen didn't seem too concerned.

Laney watched her husband's hand begin to pale to a dull yellow while the plant he was holding perked up and became a vibrant green. "I hope you don't cure all your patients that way." She knew he had given the plant new life using antibiosis transference; meaning he was draining his energy in order to restore the plant.

"Just recharging its batteries." He placed the rejuvenated plant back into the water and stepped out from behind the tank.

Laney burst out laughing.

"What's so funny?"

"What *are* you wearing?"

Allen glanced down at the broadleaf apparel wrapped around his waist. "It's a kilt. I designed it myself. What? You don't like it?"

"It's fine. I'm just used to the man-sized fig leaf."

"Well, I thought this would be more appropriate, seeing as we're about to have company."

Laney looked at her wristwatch. She had an hour before it was time to open the nursery. "You're right. Toby and Alice—"

A loud engine rumbled outside.

"—should be arriving any second," Laney finished.

Laney followed Allen to a rear door. Inside was a small room with bags stacked on two tables. Each of the forty-some bags were kilo-size and sealed in an olive green biodegradable material with the initials A&LM in a vine-like scroll.

An outside door opened.

"Ah, that feels wonderful," Allen said, spreading his arms to embrace the sunshine filtering in.

"You know, you should keep this locked," Toby Mack said, as he held the door open for Alice Kendrick. They were both in their mid-seventies, each with a youthful aura, Toby no longer incapacitated by arthritis, Alice cancer free, owing it all to Allen and his miraculous cure-all plants.

"So what do you think?" Alice asked, fluffing the back of her shoulder-length hair with her fingers and performing a cute little pirouette.

"I love it," Laney said, complimenting Alice for dying her hair from white to blond. "Makes you look ten years younger."

"Toby says it makes me look like a teenager," Alice giggled.

Laney looked at Toby. "Maybe you should shave off the facial hair before everyone thinks you're dating your daughter."

"No way," Toby said, scratching at his salt-and-pepper beard.

"Any word from the FDA and when you'll get approval?" Alice asked.

"No, I think it's going to be a while," Allen said. "We were told it could take up to three years before they conclude the laboratory testing, and then there's the application process. All we can do is keep stockpiling until the day comes."

"That's crazy," Alice said. "We have friends at the senior center who would vouch for you and tell that silly FDA how your miracle plants have improved their health and they no longer need assisted living."

"Hell, in three years you'll have enough stored up to treat the entire planet." Toby grabbed a short bundle from the table and carried it outside.

"I don't know about that," Laney said. She picked up three bags and went out to Toby's 1970 lime-green Barracuda 440. She placed the bags in the big trunk.

Allen and Alice came out with more bags.

After a couple more trips, the muscle car's trunk was full, and Toby shut the lid.

Toby opened the front passenger door.

Alice scooted onto the seat. "Thank you, young man."

"Anytime me lady," Toby grinned. He walked around the front of the car and got in behind the wheel. He started the ignition. The beefy engine roared like a trapped beast scrambling to get out from under the hood.

"Drive safely," Laney said. "Come by later this afternoon and we'll have another delivery for you."

"Sounds good. See you then," Toby said and sped off down the lane leaving a plume of trailing dust.

"They make such a nice couple," Laney said.

"What about us?" With a magician's sleight of hand, Allen created a dainty wreath of baby breath and placed it on Laney's head.

He fabricated a green ivy crown for himself.

They looked like an odd Renaissance couple.

Allen kissed Laney gently on the mouth.

When he pulled away, Laney licked her lips. "Yum, you taste minty."

8

SELF-STORAGE

As tempted as Toby was to show off the Barracuda, he made sure the muscle car never crept above the posted speed limit as they drove through town.

Alice glanced in her side mirror. "Is that black SUV following us?"

Toby looked up at the rear-view mirror and shook his head. "Nah, it's turning."

Opening the glove box, Alice took out a small booklet. She reached into her purse, and after finding a pen, made a notation on a page. "We might have to consider renting another unit soon."

"That'll mean finding another storage facility as the one we're using right now doesn't have any available units. I'm not sure Allen will like using an additional location."

"What choice do we have?"

Toby turned off the main street and drove up to a gated entrance. He reached out and punched in a number code on the access box. A second later, the ornamental iron gate slid open, giving Toby room enough to drive in.

The self-storage facility was comprised of over a hundred separate garage-style units, each with orange drop-down aluminum doors. Toby drove down a thoroughfare and turned at the first intersection, which took them to a dead end. Pulling up to the last unit, he looked over his shoulder to make sure there was no one around, and turned off the ignition.

Toby and Alice got out of the car. Toby went over and unlocked the padlock on the roll-up door. He grabbed the handle at the base and yanked the door upward so that it slid up on the track on the ceiling.

The storage unit was 10 feet by 10 feet, large enough to store three rooms of furniture.

Instead of household items, the storage unit was nearly completely filled up with stacks of bags similar to the ones that were in the Barracuda's trunk. The bags were piled up to the ceiling allowing clearance for the roll-up door and looked like a fortifying barrier of flood-impeding sandbags.

There was just enough space available to accommodate this trip and maybe one more.

Toby opened the trunk lid. "You better keep watch while I offload."

"Nonsense. Let me help," Alice said. She reached inside the cargo space and grabbed an armful of olive green bags.

"Then we better hurry," Toby said.

They worked diligently transporting the bags from the car to the storage unit.

Toby stuffed the last bundle inside. There was a gap large enough to accommodate twenty more parcels. "Well, looks like after the next run, we better find another place."

"I already made some calls," Alice said.

"You did?"

"Easy Storage on Fifth Avenue has some vacancies."

"Well, aren't you the prudent one?"

"Glad you approve."

Toby reached up and pulled down the aluminum door. He secured the padlock while Alice closed the trunk. "Where to now?" he asked as they got in the car.

"I don't care, surprise me."

"How about we say hi to the gang at the senior center and grab some lunch?"

"Fine by me."

Toby started up the Barracuda, revved the engine, and headed for the exit.

9

SUBPOENA

Nick Wells made the last pass across the front lawn and shut off the mower. He wished Gabe was still living at home; not so much that trimming the grass was his chore, but because he missed his son since he had gone off to college.

Since Gabe's recovery after having a mental breakdown due to the traumatic near-death experience the family had suffered at Cryptid Zoo, Nick and Gabe had formed a strong father and son bond.

He emptied the bag of freshly mown grass into a 30-gallon can and parked the mower in the garage. He was closing the garage door when the mail truck pulled up to the curb. The carrier shoved some correspondence into Nick's box and drove off.

Nick went down and collected his mail. He fanned through the short stack as he walked up the driveway. It was mostly junk mail, a utility bill, and an official looking envelope addressed from a District of Columbia Court. He slipped his finger under the flap and opened the envelope. He removed the folded letter and opened it up to read.

It was a subpoena requesting him to appear in Washington D.C. before a committee hearing spearheaded by Senator Jonathan Rollins. "Well, isn't this some shit."

Nick went inside the house and found his wife, Meg, preparing lunch in the kitchen. "You're not going to believe this," he said, holding up the letter.

"What do you got there?"

"It's a subpoena to appear in court."

"What in the world for?"

"They want me to testify about what happened at Cryptid Zoo. It seems there's a bill to put these creatures on the Endangered Species list. They need someone that was there first hand so they can block the bill."

"Why do they need you on a witness stand if it's all in your book?"

29

"I don't know." Nick's tell-all book, *Cryptid Hell*, depicting the horrifying weekend his family had endured trying to stay alive had done quite well sales-wise.

"When are you supposed to appear?" Meg asked.

"In two days."

"That doesn't give you much time."

"Doesn't give *us* much time you mean."

"You want me to go?"

"I certainly don't want to go by myself. Besides, you've been bugging me for a vacation."

"I don't think twiddling my thumbs in a hotel room while you're sitting in a courtroom is going to be much fun."

"Sure it will. Once it's over, we can take a shuttle flight and pay Gabe a surprise visit."

That put a smile on Meg's face. "Well, then, I guess we better start packing."

10

CRAZY DRIVER

As small-town sheriff of Rocklin Falls, Abe Stone single-handedly had the responsibility of enforcing the law and protecting the close-knit community. Even though the job could be demanding at times, it did have its perks; such as being able to have lunch with his wife, Clare, most days at their farmhouse just out of town.

A hot bowl of tomato soup and a plate of two pita pockets with circular slices of white goat cheese tucked inside were waiting for him on the kitchen table when he came in.

He glanced through the kitchen window and spotted Clare out in one of the pens, pouring feed into a trough for the goats.

Rounder, Clare's trusted Great Pyrenees Mountain Dog, stood close by her side and watched the flock milling at the feeder. Clare had raised him from a pup growing up amongst the goats so he could learn their behavioral characteristics and become a qualified Livestock Guardian Dog. Weighing 130 pounds, Rounder was a big boy with a long, white coat and thick hair around his neck to protect his throat from sharp fangs in the event he ever had to come up against a large predator, such as a wolf.

Abe sat at the table. He snatched two packets of Saltine crackers from a basket, crushed them in the palm of his hand, and tore off the corners. He sprinkled the crumbled bits into his soup. Each spoonful was hearty, as Clare always made her soups with fresh ingredients straight from their garden.

He took a bite of a pita pocket stuffed with goat cheese. It had a strong tangy taste. The faint ammonia smell filled his nostrils like he had just taken a whiff of smelling salts.

A knife was on another plate beside the partially cut cheese log half-covered with wax paper if he wanted more. He had to admit he had acquired a fondness for the robust dairy product especially after his wife and neighbor had gone into partnership. Clare provided the milking goats, and her friend, Myrtle, processed the curds into her award-winning cheeses, a match made in culinary heaven in Abe's opinion.

Abe finished up with lunch and put his plate in the sink. He covered the cheese log and placed it inside the refrigerator. The coffee maker was on and had a fresh brewed pot. He took a moment to fill his thermos and then stepped outside onto the stoop.

"Thanks for lunch," he called out.

Clare turned and gave him a warm smile. "Glad you liked it." She emptied the last of the pellets into the trough and walked over to the split rail fence.

Abe came down the steps to meet her. "How's your crew doing? Any more casualties?"

"Nope. They're all accounted for. For the time being."

"Let's hope it stays that way," Abe said. He spotted Clare's sharpshooter, a Steyr SSG Marksman leaning up against a fence post. "Expecting trouble?"

"Always, you know that."

Abe tried not to stare at the permanent scars on Clare's arms from fighting off a Chupacabra when a group had attacked her goats while camped out on a customer's property. The vile creature had pinned her to the ground and after contact, infested Clare with an extremely painful case of scabies. It was the worst the doctors had ever seen.

After two weeks in the hospital and numerous doses of invermectin, she was finally released.

Sixteen months later, he'd still catch her absentmindedly scratching at her arms as she swore she could still feel them crawling under her skin.

"Give me a call if you need me," Abe said. He hoisted his thermos in the air as a farewell and walked over to his Ford Bronco. He opened the door with the Rocklin Falls Sheriff emblem on the side and climbed behind the wheel.

Abe pulled out of the driveway and headed out onto the main road.

Everyone knew to call Abe direct if there was a problem, as he didn't have a dispatcher. He wasn't the kind of sheriff to wait for trouble to happen. He preferred to head it off whenever possible and decided to cruise the surrounding roads on the outskirts of town for any disturbances.

After being on the road for fifteen minutes, Abe came upon a straight patch. He unscrewed the cap of his thermos and placed the mug part in the cup holder. With one eye on the road, he poured himself half a cup of coffee. He placed the thermos between his thighs and screwed the cap back on. He took a small sip. It was too hot to drink so he set it in the cup holder.

The straightaway was beginning to develop into a series of windy curves as he headed up into the dense forest of junipers and ponderosa pines. He spotted a sign: Blue Ridge campground 17 miles.

Abe figured his coffee had to have cooled down and reached for it. He was lifting the cup to his lips when a moving van shot out of the trees from a dirt side road causing him to turn the wheel sharply with one hand, spilling his coffee on the front of his shirt and scolding his lap. "Son of a bitch!"

The van swerved back and forth as the driver struggled to gain control of the wheel. The vehicle picked up speed and barreled down the road.

Abe tossed the empty cup on the passenger seat. He turned on the roof lights, sounded the siren, and gunned the big engine. Abe had traveled this stretch of road many times and knew the farther up the mountain it went, the windier it became. In some cases, there were sharp hairpin turns that could only be navigated safely at 15 miles an hour.

He accelerated and pushed the Bronco's speedometer to fifty; twenty miles an hour over the posted speed limit for the treacherous country road. Abe waited until his truck was three car-lengths behind the van before he grabbed his mike from the dashboard. "You in the van! Pull over now!"

Instead of slowing down, the van kept on driving erratically, crossing over the divider and speeding up even more.

Abe glanced at the dashboard and saw he was doing sixty. At this speed he knew it was too dangerous to stay in pursuit. Sooner or later an oncoming car would come around a bend and slam head-on into the van as it was all over the road.

He smacked the top of the steering wheel with the heel of his hand and yelled, "Slow down you fool, before you kill someone!"

But it was too late.

The van leaned precariously to its left as it attempted a tight turn and went onto the shoulder, bouncing off a tree but managing to return to the pavement. A rear door flew open and a body rolled out, landing directly in the path of Abe's Bronco.

He stood on the brakes and the truck screeched to a halt.

The van disappeared around the bend and was gone.

"Crazy bastard!" Abe growled.

He opened his door, climbed out, and stomped to the front of the Bronco to see what was lying in the road.

Abe took one good look and muttered, "Holy shit!"

11

ROADKILL

Abe was sitting on the tailgate when Jack and Nora arrived. Jack parked away from the line of road flares Abe had placed on the center divider strip. Abe jumped down as they got out of their Ford Expedition.

"Sorry to call you out here but I thought you should see this," Abe said.

"That's quite all right. What do you have?" Nora asked.

"Take a look for yourself." Abe walked them around to the front of the Bronco.

"That is one big sheep," Jack said.

"I'll say," Nora confirmed. "Must have weighed close to four hundred pounds."

The animal was a ram with sawed-off horns.

Jack went down on one knee to examine the corpse. "Look at the size of those wounds." The ram had two massive chunks missing. Its entire rump and left leg were gone and there was an enormous gaping hole in its side exposing a bloodied chewed upon ribcage.

"Am I seeing this right or are those *just* two bite marks?" Abe asked.

"Appears that way." Nora pulled a measuring tape from her pocket and bent down.

"What do you think? Maybe a Bergman's bear?" Jack suggested.

"Hard to tell," Nora said. She stretched the tape across the open wound on the animal's side. "Whatever did this has a bite radius of nearly 120 degrees. That's like an anaconda."

"What, are saying a snake did this?" Abe asked.

"No." Nora leaned a little closer. "Sheriff, could you get me a pair of gloves? I think I see something."

"Sure." Abe walked around to the back of the Bronco. He reached inside and grabbed a small box out of his duty bag. He carried the box back, placed it on the hood, and pulled out a pair of plastic gloves for Nora.

Nora slipped them on. She reached inside the animal's chest cavity, felt around, and then gave a quick yank. She held up what looked like a twelve-inch long curved piece of bone.

"Is that a tooth?" Jack asked.

Abe leaned down for a better look. "From what?"

"If I didn't know any better, I'd say this came from a saber-toothed tiger," Nora said.

"What? That's crazy," Jack said.

"I know," Nora said. "They've been extinct for over 500,000 years."

12

KNACKER'S YARD

After agreeing to leave their truck at the junction where the sheriff was almost hit by the van, Nora and Jack rode with him in the Bronco.

"What's down this road, anything?" Nora asked, leaning forward in the middle of the rear seat, hands resting on the headrests of the front bucket seats so she could get a clear view through the windshield.

"Just an abandoned farm," Sheriff Stone said. "Road comes out ten miles on the other side of town."

"Any idea what the van might have been doing down here?" Jack asked, sitting in the front passenger seat. He was armed with his holstered revolver and the hunting rifle he always kept handy in a special compartment in the back of the Expedition.

"Only that he was in a damn hurry," the sheriff replied.

"Probably trying to outrun you," Nora said.

"No, he was driving like a maniac before he saw me."

Ever since they had started down the road, the sheriff kept his speed at a constant twenty miles an hour, slow enough so they could keep a lookout for anything suspicious in the nearby trees and shrubs off the side of the road.

"Is that the property you were talking about?" Nora asked when she spotted a rundown farmhouse up ahead. Sections of the roof had rotted and collapsed into the decrepit structure. The chimney was a ruin surrounded by uneven piles of fallen bricks.

"That's it," the sheriff replied.

A rutty road ran behind the farmhouse deeper into the trees.

"Think we should check back there?" Nora said.

"Sure, best to cover all the bases," Sheriff Stone said. He slowed the Bronco and turned down the rough road. Nora and Jack held on, jostled by every bounce and dip as the all-terrain tires rolled in and out of the potholes.

They had gone a hundred feet when Jack shouted, "Stop! I think I saw something."

The sheriff put on the brakes. "Where?"

"Over there," Jack said, pointing to a small clearing mostly hidden behind the dense foliage.

The sheriff shut off the engine.

Jack climbed out of the Bronco. He tilted the passenger seat forward so Nora could step out from the back.

Sheriff Stone grabbed his Remington pump shotgun from the mounting rack. He opened the console between the bucket seats and took out a box of shells. He grabbed a handful of cartridges and stuffed them in his coat pocket.

"So what do you think you saw?" the sheriff asked Jack as he fed cartridges into the shotgun's chamber.

"Not sure. Something lying out there in the grass." Jack cradled his hunting rifle over the crook of his arm.

"Let's go take a look." Sheriff Stone took the lead. Jack and Nora followed close behind. Nora didn't draw her sidearm but kept her hand on the grip.

They stepped through the trees and came to a small grassy meadow that may have been used for grazing at one time.

Nora was the first one to spot the mangled body. "Oh my God."

"Jesus, will you look at that," the sheriff said.

It was really nothing more than chewed up grisly flesh and jagged bone sticking out of shredded clothing lying in a pool of blood. A crimson halo of blood splattered the surrounding blades of grass.

Nora heard movement on the other side of the bramble maybe twenty feet away. "There's something behind that brush." She drew her gun.

Sheriff Stone and Jack pointed their weapons at the shrubbery.

A saber-toothed tiger stepped out from behind the entanglement. It had matted brown fur with a dirty white chest and a short tail, bony shoulders, ribs jutting from its emaciated body and should have weighed in the vicinity of 800 pounds per the textbooks but in its malnourished state was half that weight. Its mouth hung open, revealing a single tusk-like fang.

"What's wrong with it?" Sheriff Stone whispered to Nora.

"It's sick."

So far, the tiger showed no sign of sensing they were there. It took a couple of unsure steps, stopped, and kept facing away from them.

The tiger's belly contracted and it made a coughing, gagging sound then disgorged the contents of its stomach onto the ground.

Nora saw a severed human hand amongst the bile.

The tiger turned its head and looked directly at them.

"Oh, shit," Sheriff Stone said, raising the shotgun barrel.

Jack and Nora aimed their guns, expecting the tiger to charge at any moment.

The big cat took one more step and then dropped flat on its belly onto the ground, its head lulling to one side. Its thick tongue unfurled out of its mouth onto the dirt.

"What the hell?" Jack said.

They warily approached the animal.

Nora didn't know if the creature was playing possum and might leap at them suddenly, but it remained still. "I think it's dead."

"I don't get it. It just made a meal out of that guy," Jack said. "What the hell happened here?"

Nora looked at Jack and the sheriff. "My guess is they came here to dispose of the tiger thinking it was already dead."

"And then one of them was attacked," Jack chimed in.

"That makes sense," Sheriff Stone said. "The other guy panicked and left his buddy behind."

"But why here?" Jack said.

Nora glanced at the surrounding trees. "Maybe we should take a look around?"

"Best stay together," the sheriff suggested.

"Fine by me," Nora said.

They started walking through the shin-high grass in the direction of the trees further behind the abandoned farmhouse, and hadn't gone more than twenty yards, when Nora caught a putrid whiff of something ahead. She could hear the drone of buzzing flies.

"Ah, man," Jack said, covering his nose and mouth.

"Looks like a damn slaughterhouse," the sheriff said.

The revolting site was enough to make them cringe. Nora figured there had to be scores of rotting carcasses in different stages of decomposition. Some bloated from built-up internal gases, others nothing more than parched bone.

"Someone's been dumping these animals for sometime," Nora said. Even though some of the remains were almost unrecognizable she could tell by the bone structures that they were not domestic animals.

"Is that what I think it is?" Jack asked as he pointed to one of the dead creatures.

"You mean a Chupacabra?"

Jack nodded.

"That would be my guess," Nora said. The oval shaped head was still intact but the spiny back and gangly legs were withered. She saw what was left of a young Thunderbird; its feathers shriveled away, a small mound of bones from past meals where its stomach once was.

What at first glance looked like the remains of a bear cub was really a mangy Bigfoot left to rot alongside the other carcasses.

"What do you make of it, Professor?" the sheriff asked.

"I believe we're looking at what's called a knacker's yard. It's an old British expression. It's a place used for disposing animal carcasses. Obviously someone's been dumping these creatures here; whether they were alive or dead at the time would be difficult to determine even with an examination."

"And you think Dr. McCabe is behind this?" the sheriff asked.

"Who else? I think he's lost the recipe."

"What are you saying?" Jack asked.

"I'm saying, he's making defective cryptids prone to disease."

"Why dump them out here?"

"Maybe he's worried of contaminating the others."

"Which raises another question," the sheriff said.

"What's that?" Nora asked.

"Where did that van come from?"

13

RABBIT HOLE

Lyle Mason drove the van with one hand, keeping his left arm elevated on the driver's door so he wouldn't bleed to death. The cab's interior looked like the inside of an abattoir; his clothes, the floor mats, and the seats covered with his blood. Stabbing pain shot the length of his arm like sharp daggers raking his flesh. His blood-soaked shirtsleeve was torn in places giving him glimpses of the deep oozing wounds. It was a miracle the big cat hadn't ripped his arm clean off.

Damn thing was supposed to have been dead.

He had no idea how much blood was inside a human body, but by the gory mess surrounding him it seemed he had bled enough for two people.

Mason hated leaving Billy behind but he knew his helper was dead. It was best to get out of there as fast as possible. He didn't see any point in the both of them ending up as the saber-tooth's meal ticket. It was bad enough having to haul the stinky things out to the dumping ground let alone being attacked by something that was supposed to be on the verge of dying.

Mason had been driving for over an hour since evading the sheriff. It was dumb luck the stupid sheep falling out the back.

Mason caught himself nodding off and snapped awake.

He was losing too much blood.

The stretch of road ahead had straightened out as he sped through the forest. He kept his eyes peeled for the bogus road marker, praying he hadn't already passed it.

And then he spotted the sign off the side of the road: CB-17

Mason slowed the van and turned off the asphalt onto the dirt road that led deeper into the woods. He traveled through the forest and came to a gate blocking the road. He stopped, pushed a button on the sun visor, and the gate swung open. He drove on through, hitting the remote. He glanced at the side mirror and made sure the gate closed behind him.

He kept going for a short distance, reaching what appeared to be a dead end and a stand of trees blocking the road.

Mason accelerated.

The tree trunks loomed through the windshield.

He clutched the steering wheel with his right hand and braced himself.

Just before the imminent impact, the nose of the van pitched downward and the vehicle shot through an underground tunnel. Overhead lights lit up, triggered as the van passed through.

The borehole was nearly twenty feet in diameter and extended for a quarter mile.

Mason was relieved to see the trucks parked up ahead in the underground garage. He pulled up beside a van similar to his and shut off the engine.

He opened the driver door with his right hand and screamed from the excruciating pain when his left arm fell down by his side. Unsure if he could even stand, Mason grabbed the door with his right hand and slipped off the driver seat. His knees buckled when his boots hit the cement but he managed to stay on his feet.

He shuffled toward a large metal door and stared up at the surveillance camera.

Mason pressed the call box. "It's Lyle Mason. I need help."

Seconds later, the heavy security door opened.

Two guards with carbines stepped out, followed by three men dressed in white medical smocks, pushing a gurney. They helped Mason onto the gurney and wheeled him inside. Lying flat on his back, he could hear the clunk of the door closing.

The overhead lights were bright as he was transported down the corridor.

On either side of him were glass windows revealing various laboratories. He could hear the faint wails and screeches of the animal experiments.

Mason was ready to pass out when the medical team brought him into a surgical theater. He could hear the snip of the scissors cutting away his shirt and voices rattling off medical jargon.

A figure stood in the doorway.

It was the fiendish Dr. McCabe.

Someone stuck a needle into Mason's arm and he quickly drifted off.

14

SEIZURE

It was nearly evening and getting chilly so Toby decided to put the top up on the Barracuda despite Alice's claim she wasn't cold. Even though Allen's cure-all plants had restored Toby and Alice's health and they no longer suffered from their debilitating illnesses, it didn't mean they were invulnerable. Being in their mid-seventies, they still had to manage their wellness.

Toby turned at the light and headed toward the entrance to the public storage facility. Stopping at the gate, he entered the code on the touch pad. The iron barrier opened and he drove through.

"I think once we're through here, we should swing by Easy Storage and sign up for a space," Alice said.

"Good idea. Get it out of the way," Toby replied, turning to follow the lane down between the storage units. He stopped at the last garage unit.

Toby got out. He walked to the trunk, slipped in the key, and opened the lid.

The cargo area was filled with bags of the cure-all plants.

He poked his head around the side of the car and said to Alice as she was getting out, "Stand watch while I unlock the unit."

"Sure thing, Mr. Paranoia." Alice smirked with an eye roll.

"Hey, this is serious business."

"It's not like we're doing anything illegal."

"It's beginning to feel that way, the way we're always sneaking around." Toby walked over to the closed aluminum door. He bent down to unlock the padlock. "This isn't good."

"What's wrong?" Alice asked and stepped toward Toby.

"Someone cut the lock." Toby removed the severed padlock. He grabbed the bottom lip and raised the roll-up door.

The storage unit had been cleaned out except for maybe fifty bags.

"Think I'm paranoid now?"

"Oh my God," Alice gasped.

"I can't believe it," Toby said, shaking his head. "Allen and Laney are going to totally freak out. We've been at this for more than six months."

"Who do you think it was?"

"I have *no* idea. It's not like we were hiding drugs," Toby said.

"Maybe someone has been watching us and thought we were."

Toby glanced around, searching for a vantage point where someone might have been spying on them from a distance. A waterproof canvas covered the ten-foot tall chain-link fence topped with razor wire that ran from their storage unit and across the lane to the other unit so there was no way anyone could see inside from outside the compound unless they had used a drone.

"Maybe it was an inside job," Toby said, spotting a surveillance camera mounted a few units away near the roof.

"You seriously think the owner ripped us off?"

"Sure, why—"

A black cargo van raced around the corner and barreled towards them.

"Look out," Toby said and pulled Alice out of the path of the vehicle as it skidded to a halt.

The back doors flew open and six men in ski masks dressed in black stormed out.

Four ran into the garage while a man stood pointing an automatic pistol at Toby and Alice.

"What the hell is going on? Who are you people?" Toby shouted.

"Quiet and you won't get hurt."

"What is this, some kind of bust?"

"Don't make me laugh," the gun-wielding man said.

Toby noticed one of the men standing on the other side of the Barracuda. "Hey, buddy, what the hell are you doing?" Toby shouted.

The man rushed back to the passenger side of the van.

Toby watched the other men come out of the garage, carrying armfuls of bags. "Now, wait one God damn minute." He went to stop the man nearest him.

"Stay put, I'm warning you." The man with the gun cocked the hammer.

"Toby, please," Alice said, clinging to Toby's arm. "I think he means it."

"We can't just stand by and let them get away with this."

"I don't see we have a choice."

The men made two more trips from the garage to the van until the unit was completely empty. They climbed into the back of the van.

The man with the gun stepped backwards, never taking his eyes off of Toby and Alice then turned quickly and joined the others.

The driver of the van drove in reverse to the junction, turned, and sped off toward the exit.

"Come on, we can't let them get away." Toby ran for the car while Alice went around to her side.

"Oh no!" Alice said.

"What is it?" Toby asked, opening his door.

"You have two flats."

"You have got to be kidding me." Toby raced around the car. "So that's what that guy was doing. Letting the air out of my tires. Good thing I have a battery-operated pump."

"What are we going to tell Allen and Laney?" Alice said. "They're going to be devastated."

"Don't worry, we're not beaten yet."

"What do you mean?"

"I memorized the license plate number."

15

FOOD CART

Nick had booked a late morning flight for Washington D.C. so they wouldn't have to contend with the heavy commuter traffic even though they were taking Uber to the airport. He figured the less hassle the better.

"I can't believe you talked me into taking only one suitcase," Meg said, as they stood second in line at the check-in counter.

"Why pay fifty bucks for an extra bag? Besides, we have our carry-ons."

"If you say so, Mr. Frugal."

"Just call a duck a duck."

"Okay, you're a cheapskate."

"Feel better now?" Nick said as they moved up to the counter.

"Can I have your confirmations?" the ticket agent asked.

"Sure." Nick handed the young woman the printouts he had generated from his home computer.

She reviewed the paperwork, placed their tickets in a boarding pass, and after affixing the destination tags on the handle, she placed the large suitcase on the scale. "I'm sorry but your bag exceeds our weight limit. There will be an additional charge of fifty dollars."

"What?" Nick said.

"You can pay with a credit card."

Nick looked at Meg. "I don't believe this."

"In for a penny, in for an ounce," Meg said with a smirk.

Nick handed over his credit card. The ticket agent concluded the transaction, returned Nick's card, and placed the suitcase on the conveyor belt moving behind her.

Nick watched their bag disappear through an opening with hanging strips of black rubber.

"You'll be departing at Gate Number 7. Enjoy your flight," the ticket agent said.

"Yeah, thanks," Nick grumbled and slipped the boarding passes into the side pocket of his sports jacket.

They walked through the terminal and took their place at the end of the line for the TSA checkpoint.

"Shoot," Nick said.

"What's wrong?"

"Do we have to take our shoes off?"

"Of course," Meg said. "Don't tell me you're wearing that pair of socks with the hole in the toe."

Nick gave her a sheepish grin.

"Seriously?"

"No, I'm just kidding."

"Idiot."

Nick figured there had to be over fifty people ahead of them. He looked over his shoulder and saw twenty more behind and the line steadily growing.

He felt like they were being bunched together like cattle while those at the head of the line were being processed slowly through the TSA scanners.

And then the most unimaginable thing happened.

Meg pinched her nose and looked at him.

"Are you crying?" he asked, noticing Meg's eyes watering.

"No," she replied with a nasal twang. "Can't you smell it?"

Nick took a whiff and quickly covered his nose. "Jesus, that's rank." He almost wanted to say, "Who the hell just farted?" but knew he better not. Typically the person that made such a comment was the culprit trying to avert the blame onto someone else.

If he ever felt trapped, this was the time. Nick glanced around and briefly studied the faces to see if he could detect the person who had cut loose but everyone seemed to be keeping a straight face. No one seemed to be reacting to the smell.

"Guess we'll just have to grin and bear it," Nick whispered to Meg.

Finally the air cleared and ten minutes later they were next in line to be scanned.

They took off their shoes and put them on the X-ray conveyor along with their carry-on bags. Nick emptied his pockets and put everything into a small tray along with Meg's purse that also went through the machine.

Meg raised her arms shoulder height while the TSA agent used a handheld wand to scan her body. When no alarms went off, Nick stepped up next. The agent swept the wand over Nick's right arm and down his waist along the outside of his right leg and then up the inside to his groin, repeating the motion on the other side of his body.

"Keep going," the agent said.

As an added precaution, Nick and Meg were also required to stand in the full-body scanner, which was a gray contraption that looked like a narrow doorway leading into a portal to another dimension.

Once they had gone through and were given the "all clear", Nick and Meg put on their shoes. Nick collected his belongings from the tray while Meg grabbed her purse and both of their carry-on bags.

They continued on to their designated departure gate.

"Security seems pretty tight around here," Nick said, spotting two-man teams dressed in camouflage fatigues and carrying military-assault weapons, patrolling the terminal.

"Fine by me," Meg said. "Remember those people that were attacked by those things at LAX?"

"Oh yeah. And I thought it was bad enough having to worry about a terrorist threat." Nick spotted their gate number. People were filing through the entrance of the enclosed passenger boarding bridge to the airplane.

Nick and Meg got in line and edged their way into the tube to the open hatchway.

"Welcome aboard," the young flight attendant greeted.

"Thank you," Meg said.

Nick nodded with a smile. He got behind Meg and they made their way up the aisle, having to stop every couple of feet, hampered by passengers blocking the way as they stowed their carry-ons in the overhead storage compartments.

"Where are our seats?" Meg asked, unable to disguise the irritability in her voice.

"We're second to the last row."

"All the way in the back!"

"Meg, it's proven the safest place to be is in the back of the plane in the event of a crash." Nick glanced down and saw a little girl in her seat, staring up at him. It was obvious the worried look on her face meant she had overheard him. He smiled at her and shook his head. "Just kidding."

They continued on at a snail pace.

"If it will make you feel better," Nick said, "you can have the middle seat for added protection."

Meg glanced back at him. "Next you'll have us wearing helmets and shoulder pads."

"Actually, that might not be a bad idea." Nick checked the boarding passes and looked over at the row of vacant seats near the lavatory. "Those are our seats."

Nick let Meg slide in first while he put their carry-ons in the overhead bin. He noticed that all of the storage bin doors had been left open. He figured once everyone was seated, the flight attendant would go down the aisle and close the doors.

Instead of occupying the middle seat, Meg chose to sit by the window. Nick had no problem sitting in the middle seat next to her.

He glanced over the seat headrest and saw a flight attendant standing in the galley. The rear hatch door was open so the food service workers could wheel in carts filled with already-prepared meals for the flight.

"That's not safe," Nick said.

"What isn't?" Meg asked, staring out the window at the tarmac.

"Keeping the door open like that. They have all this ridiculous security inside the terminal but don't care when it comes to protecting passengers on the planes?"

"I'm sure they know what they're doing."

"I think I'm going to say something." Nick rose from his seat and started for the aisle.

"No, you don't," Meg said, reaching out and grabbing his arm. "Sit down. The quicker they're done, the quicker we take off."

"I still don't like it." Nick was taking a step back to return to his seat when the flight attendant screamed. He turned to the galley and saw a food service worker with something that looked like a fleshy turban wrapped around his entire head. The man was struggling to remove the thing. Nick could hear his muffled pleas for help.

A snakehead rose six inches from his scalp, opened its mouth wide, and sank its fangs into the man's scalp.

The man's hands immediately dropped limply to his side and he collapsed but not before the flying snake unfurled its four wings and flew into the aircraft cabin.

Nick ducked as it went down the aisle and soared past the other passengers. He recognized the creature as he had seen similar reptiles during his fateful weekend at Cryptid Zoo. It was an Arabhar, a legendary flying snake thought to inhabit areas near the Arabian Sea. The snake was dangerous and extremely poisonous.

People were swatting at the flying snake with in-flight magazines or cowering in their seats with their hands over their heads.

The deadly snake landed on a man's shoulder and bit him in the face.

It took mere seconds for the man to succumb to the quick-acting venom. He slumped forward, fell out of his seat, and landed face down in the aisle, creating a pandemonium of high-pitched screams.

Nick leaned out and peered down the aisle.

The snake swooped about the cabin and landed on the seat back directly in front of the little girl Nick had spoken to earlier. She took one horrified look at the snake and covered her head with her arms.

Nick jumped out into the aisle and yelled. "Everyone be quiet!"

Many of the passengers looked at Nick like he was crazy but lowered their voices.

"Let me see if I can draw it out!" Nick looked to his left and saw a pillow and folded blanket in one of the overhead storage bins. He grabbed the blanket and shook it out then threw it down on the seat. He snatched the pillow out and began to wave it around to attract the snake, figuring it might think it was some kind of prey it could sink its teeth into. "Hey over here! Come and get it!"

The snake was hissing at the little girl when it noticed the white object moving about down the aisle. Temptations being too great, the Arabhar lunged off the seat back and flew directly at Nick.

"Oh my God, Nick!" Meg yelled.

Nick held the pillow shoulder height, waiting for the precise moment.

Before the snake could attack, Nick swung the pillow and knocked the snake into the open storage bin. He snatched the loose blanket and tossed it over the flailing reptile then slammed the door shut.

Everyone on board turned in their seats and gave him a loud round of applause.

Nick gazed at the dead man in the middle of the aisle, knowing there was another one lying in the galley.

"Ladies and gentlemen," the captain's voice boomed over the cabin's intercom. "We ask that you leave any personal belongings currently in the overhead bins and disembark in an orderly fashion through the front of the plane. We apologize for the inconvenience."

The passengers got out of their seats and funneled awkwardly into the aisle. A few looked back at Nick with appreciative smiles and gave him a thumbs up.

Meg stood and moved next to Nick. "Honey, you were amazing."

The Arabhar thrashed inside the closed overhead bin.

Nick turned to Meg. "Yeah, you might say I'm quite the snake charmer."

16

BAG LUNCH

Toby revved the Barracuda's throaty engine and shut off the ignition. He got out of the car, went around to the passenger side, and opened the door.

"Thank you, garcon," Alice said as she got out.

"You do know garcon means waiter," Toby said.

"Oh? I thought it meant valet."

"Very funny."

They strolled arm in arm up the sloped wheelchair accessible walkway to the front doors of the senior center.

"I still think we need to call Allen and Laney," Alice said.

"And tell them what? That we let some jerks steal their plants. They trusted us. I think I may have a way to get them back."

"And that's why we're here?"

"Yeah. And the free food." Toby held the glass door for Alice as they went inside.

"Morning Lucy," Toby greeted the stocky woman standing behind the main desk.

"Well hello, Toby. Alice. Are you here for the bag lunch?"

Alice smiled at the director.

"You bet," Toby replied.

"Enjoy."

Months ago when they would come to the senior center, Toby and Alice would see residents still in their pajamas and robes, slumped in their wheelchairs, parked in the hallway. Those with gumption enough to get out of bed could be found in the recreation room, some with their heads down on the tables, others sitting like zombies because they had been over medicated. Many preferred to just stay in their rooms.

Today there were no wheelchairs in the hallway.

Toby could hear voices down the corridor and went to the doorway of the recreation room to look in.

Thirty elderly people sat at tables, eating sandwiches and fruit snacks and drinking juice boxes taken from the brown paper bags in front of them.

Everyone beamed with happy smiles, engaging in cheery conversations with those at their table. They were all taking Allen's home remedy for one ailment or another and had been cured thanks to his plants. The only reason they were staying in the nursing facility was so they could remain with their friends, as many of them had nowhere else to go.

For Lucy it was a dream come true. She was able to cut her staff from fifteen down to two people, as the residents were all self-sufficient and no longer had to be given baths and have their soiled linens changed. They pretty much looked out for each other and ran the place on their own.

Everything was copacetic as long as the checks came rolling in on the first day of every month.

A burly man, with long gray hair braided in a ponytail, raised his hand and beckoned Toby and Alice over to his table. The couple grabbed a bag lunch each from the serving table and went over to sit down.

"How are things, Harvey?" Toby asked, shaking the man's hand.

"Not bad, not bad at all."

"You're looking well," Alice said, opening her bag.

"Thanks to you two, I'm still cancer free."

"Well, I wish we could take the credit." Alice unwrapped her sandwich. She lifted the corner of the top slice to inspect the makings. "Pimento loaf, yuck. Does anyone care to trade?"

Toby looked inside his sandwich. "Do you want liverwurst?"

Alice furrowed her brow.

"I can give you half of mine," Harvey said.

"What do you have?"

"Head cheese on pumpernickel."

"Oh, that's disgusting." Alice swapped sandwiches with Toby.

Halfway through their meal, Toby asked Harvey, "Does your son still work for the DMV?"

"Sure does," Harvey replied between chews.

"Think I could ask a favor?"

"Whatever you need. Ask away."

"I need a name and address for a license plate. Think he can do that?"

"Let me finish up and I'll give him a call."

"Thanks, Harvey."

"For you, man. Anything. Just don't ask me to bump someone off."

"Promise."

17

SLEUTHS

"Well that doesn't give us much of a lead," Alice said as they walked to the car having finished their lunch at the senior center.

Toby held up the notepad page Harvey had used to jot down the information supplied by his son at the DMV. "True, an address would have been more useful. That's the trouble when a vehicle is registered to a big corporation like Wilde Enterprises though I doubt we'd find that van parked in the corporate headquarters parking lot."

"Isn't the corporate office somewhere back east?"

"That's right," Toby said. "Clear across the country."

"So what dealings does Wilde Enterprises have out here?" Alice asked as she slipped past Toby and climbed into the front passenger seat of the Barracuda.

Toby closed Alice's door. He walked around the back of the car and got behind the wheel. "That's a good question. Did you bring your Paddy with you?"

"Yes, it's right here." Alice reached inside her purse and took out her iPad.

"Go on the Wilde Enterprises website and see if they have a branch or division around here?" Toby sat back in his seat and waited while Alice booted up her handheld computer. He turned his head and let out an indiscreet burp.

"I heard that," Alice said, staring down at the small screen.

"I can't help it. Olive loaf always gets to me."

"You know, you didn't have to trade."

"Trade or not, it doesn't matter. Liverwurst gives me gas, too."

"I may have found something. Take a look." Alice handed the iPad to Toby.

Toby took a moment to read the website. "It's worth a try." He handed Alice back the device, started the muscle car, and sped out of the parking lot.

It took them thirty minutes on the freeway before reaching their destination.

From the street, the three-story building looked like a hospital adjoined to a massive warehouse, the complex surrounded by a twelve-foot high chain-link fence.

Two guards in uniform were posted at the single entrance accessing the property.

"That looks like the only way in," Toby said as they drove slowly by.

"So now what?" Alice asked, slouched in her seat so as not to be seen.

"Well, we could take the direct approach and drive up to the guard shack."

"And tell them what? We think some of your guys broke into our storage unit and we want our stuff back?"

"I doubt if it would be that easy. I have another idea." Toby accelerated down the street and made the first turn which took them down a tree line stretch obscuring the facility. He parked at the curb and shut off the engine.

"What now?" Alice asked.

"Feel like going for a short hike?"

"Sure, I'm wearing my sensible shoes."

Toby and Alice got out of the Barracuda. They started up a grassy knoll toward a stand of eucalyptus trees. Toby glanced over his shoulder. "Nobody better mess with my car."

"I'm sure it will be fine. We won't be that long, right?"

"Not planning on it."

It took a minute to walk through the trees before they saw the building again. They had a side view of an outdoor eating area with chairs and tables with umbrellas. There was no one in sight.

Black vans similar to the one that had been at the public storage facility were parked behind the warehouse. Each vehicle was backed into a parking lot stall with the rear bumper facing the cyclone fence.

Toby took the piece of paper out of his shirt pocket. "Come on. Let's see if we can find a match."

"I'll keep a lookout while you check," Alice said. "Don't you think it's a little strange there's no one back here?"

"Keep an eye out for surveillance cameras." Toby crept along the chain-link fence looking for the license plate that corresponded with the number on the scrap piece of paper in his hand.

"Toby, I see a camera."

"Where?"

"Over by those big doors."

"Stay down." Toby lowered to a crouch and snuck behind the vans.

"This isn't exactly doing wonders for my knees," Alice balked as she followed Toby in the same fashion.

"Hey, I found it." Toby pointed to the license plate and looked at Alice.

"Bingo! Now what?"

"Let's go back to the car and figure what to do. Hopefully Allen's plants are still here." Toby turned and Alice followed him back through the trees.

"I still think we should tell Allen and Laney."

"Not yet." Toby helped Alice up the grassy knoll.

As soon as they reached the crest, Toby looked down at the street and burst out, "Son of a bitch!"

The Barracuda was gone.

18

MILKING STAND

The majority of Clare's one hundred and twenty-five goats were used for grazing farmers and ranchers' properties overrun with noxious weeds and bushes harmful to cattle and other large livestock but delicacies for a herd of goats.

Clare had a good-sized operation behind the farmhouse. Besides the five outdoor pens, she also had a twenty-foot wide by forty-foot long shed with a corrugated roof and sidewalls with four-foot clearances to the fifteen-foot tall ceiling, which allowed for adequate air circulation and reduced the barnyard smell considerably.

Since starting a partnership business with Myrtle Cooper, a state fair blue ribbon award winner, Clare had acquired twenty dairy goats so she could supply milk to her friend who processed the lactation liquid into her delicious goat cheese.

To aid in this venture, Clare had constructed a dairy goat-milking stand. The simple structure platform was made up of two-by-fours, 24 inches wide and four feet long for the animal to stand on and was elevated 12 inches off the ground. A horizontal board was bolted to the two upright braces with a pair of adjustable slats that closed around the neck with a feed box on the other end. Even though the goat's head was the only part of its body locked in so it couldn't move around, the animal was generally content as long as there was food for it to eat.

As Clare was a one-woman operation, it was often difficult to perform certain tasks all by herself. As she could not afford to hire anyone, she often had to wait until

Abe was available to help out but lately he had been too busy.

The milking stand proved to be the perfect solution.

Not only did she utilize the contraption to milk her diary goats, she used it for administering liquid worming solutions orally to the animals, giving vaccinations, and trimming their hooves, which she was currently doing to one of her does. Besides a healthy diet, it was important to keep the hooves clean and trimmed as neglect to do so on a monthly basis could lead to hoof rot and other serious problems.

Lifting the right hind leg, Clare clutched the limb firmly in one gloved hand while she used a pair of straight blade garden shears to clip the bottom and shape the cloven hoof. She dug out dirt and pebbles with the closed blades.

Once she felt the hoof was clean and well shaped, she moved onto the other hind leg. Only this time the doe was not as cooperative and began to dance around.

"Easy there," Clare said in a soothing voice. She let go of the leg and began to stroke the goat's side to calm her down. The goat stopped clopping on the wooden platform.

Rounder strolled out from the entrance of the shed. He stopped a few feet away from the milking stand and took a moment to shake the dust from his thick, white coat.

"I'm not paying you to nap," Clare said.

Rounder gave her a puzzled look, turned, and ambled back inside the shed.

"Okay, let's try this again." Before Clare could grip the doe's leg, the goats inside the shed began to bleat nervously.

Rounder joined in with his booming barks.

Clare dropped the shears on the platform. She laid her fingers on the handgrip of her father's Ruger holstered on her hip and walked slowly toward the shed entrance.

As she stepped inside, she could see some of the goats in the shadows rushing the metal fencing, others moving in huddled groups away from a mysterious threat that only they could sense.

Even if a large predator had managed to wander in, Clare would never have heard it with all the noise the goats were making and Rounder's resonate barking.

She wanted to yell for them to shut up which was as pointless as expecting storm waves to crash silently on a rocky shore.

Then came a loud crash, like a giant fist had slammed down on the top of the corrugated roof. Another bang shook the shed walls.

"Rounder! Come!" Clare shouted.

Rounder immediately ran toward her. As he reached her side, the dog growled viciously and glared at the opened doorway of the shed.

Clare turned slowly, her hand gripping her sidearm.

She gazed outside. "What the hell?"

The doe and the milking stand were no longer there.

19

COMING CLEAN

Toby felt emasculated driving Alice's wimpy Toyota Corolla instead of his beefy Barracuda but he didn't let on that it bothered him.

It could have been worse; Alice could be the one driving.

Once they had discovered that someone had stolen Toby's car, Alice called for an Uber driver to pick them up and take them to her house. After some deliberation, Toby and Alice decided to come clean and visit Laney and Allen.

Turning into the nursery parking lot, Toby shut the engine off at the front entrance.

Two other cars were in the lot; a pickup truck and an old model station wagon.

Toby and Alice sat in the car and waited for the customers to leave.

Soon a man came out pushing a cart filled with potted plants. He went over to the station wagon, opened the rear hatch, and loaded the back. He left the cart by the side of his car, got in, and drove off.

A few minutes later, a woman exited the nursery, carrying a bag of fertilizer. She walked up to the truck. She flipped the sack into the cargo bed. She climbed into the cab, started the engine, and headed off toward the main road.

"Coast is clear," Alice said.

Toby and Alice got out of the compact sedan and went inside where it was humid from the evaporating moisture of the freshly watered plants.

"Maybe she's in her office," Alice said as they walked down a row of tall ferns and potted palms.

Toby poked his head in the doorway of the Tuff Shed that served as Laney's office, consisting of a chair, desk, and a couple of filing cabinets. "She's not in here."

Alice looked at her wristwatch. "It's nearly closing time for the nursery."

"Then she's either in the back or she took a quick run over to the greenhouse."

"Let's go see." Alice walked through the nursery and out the back with Toby.

A path led through the trees for a short distance then forked in two directions, the left toward the Moss's cottage, the other way leading to the greenhouse.

Toby and Alice kept to the right. They followed the trail, which led to the greenhouse front entrance.

Alice was about to step inside when Toby pulled her back by the arm. "Not so fast. We have to announce ourselves."

"Oh my God, I forgot," Alice said, a sudden look of fear on her face.

Toby stood just outside the threshold and called in, "Laney! Allen! It's Toby and Alice!"

Laney appeared from behind a raised flowerbed. "Hi, guys. What are you doing here? We weren't expecting you until tomorrow."

"There's been a bit of a problem," Toby said. "Can we come in?"

"Ah, yes. One moment." Laney approached the doorway and stopped to look up at the two 12-foot tall man-eating trees standing sentry on either side of the entrance. The carnivorous guards had twisted their trunks, ready to snare the intruders with their giant hand-shaped branches.

Laney rubbed her hemp bracelet on her wrist, releasing the pheromone to dissuade the monstrous plants from attacking. "Easy, boys. These are our friends."

The man-eating trees immediately stood down and resumed their natural posts like a pair of bookends.

"Come in," Laney beckoned. "Allen's in the back. Stay close behind me."

Alice and Toby entered. They did as instructed and followed Laney, never once lagging more than an arm's-length away.

Walking between the raised beds, Toby kept his arms close to his sides so the taunting creeper vines twisting in the air like thin sinister serpents wouldn't grab him.

He spotted a large pitcher plant with a deep-throated bowl and swore he heard something squeal down in the pitfall trap. He glanced up and saw strangler vines hanging from the glass-paneled ceiling.

Even though most of the vegetation inside the greenhouse was grown for purely medicinal purposes, there was a deadly garrison of plants that Allen could unleash on anyone foolish enough to threaten the Moss's business.

They were almost to the door that led to the back room when Toby saw something so strange he could not believe what he was seeing.

It was Allen—or what he believed to be Laney's husband—having what seemed to be an intimate moment with a prickly ash. Tiny thorns bulged out of the green flesh of his fingers as he caressed the sharp spines on the stalks.

"Toby and Alice are here," Laney said.

Allen spun around like he had been caught doing something lurid. Blushing, Allen's face and body turned from an emerald shade to a dark forest green.

"Sorry, we didn't mean to startle you," Toby apologized.

"It's all right," Allen said. "I can get a little carried away with my work."

"So, you guys haven't told us why you're here," Laney said.

Toby glanced at Alice before saying, "Someone broke into the storage unit."

"What?" Laney gasped.

"They took everything," Toby said.

"Son of a bitch," Allen snarled.

"That's not all," Alice said. "Someone stole Toby's car."

"Oh, this keeps getting better and better," Allen said with disbelief. "Any ideas who may have done it?"

"We got a lead on a license plate," Toby said. "A van at a facility about an hour from here. A branch of Wilde Pharmaceuticals."

"Why am I not surprised?" Allen said.

"What are we going to do?" Laney asked.

"How long before it gets dark?"

Alice looked at her wristwatch. "Maybe two hours."

"I've been cooped up inside all day," Allen said. "I better go outside and sit in the sun and recharge my batteries."

"Then what?" Toby asked.

"Then we get back what's rightfully ours."

20

LOCKSMITH

Allen sat up front while Toby drove the Corolla. Laney and Alice were in the backseat sharing a blanket draped over their laps.

"I could crank up the heater," Toby said.

"No, we're fine," Alice replied.

"It's better to be safe than sorry." Allen dangled his arm out as they raced down the freeway doing sixty-miles an hour at eight o'clock in the evening with all four windows down.

"Allen's right," Laney said. "During the day he's safe to be around as his body is releasing oxygen into the air and he absorbs carbon dioxide. Just like all plants do. But at night, his body does the opposite. It sucks up oxygen and expels carbon dioxide."

"Which is why it's best we drive with the windows down," Allen said. As clothes would hinder his ability to effectively excrete the toxic waste, Allen chose to be naked, covering his body discretely with a thin bark-like armor, not so much for a defense mechanism, but so as not to make his elderly friends feel uncomfortable. "You wouldn't want to be stuck with me in tight quarters at nighttime."

"Why, did something happen?" Alice asked.

"When Allen first began to change," Laney said, "I almost died from asphyxiation while we were sleeping together. Luckily, Allen realized what was happening and was able to revive me."

"That sucks." Toby turned onto an off-ramp and went down a few streets before stopping at the curb at the same spot where the Barracuda had been stolen. "This is where we had parked before."

"Probably not a good idea to leave the car here too long." Allen turned in his seat and looked at Laney. "Might be better if you stay with Alice. Toby and I will go check it out."

"Okay," Laney said.

Allen and Toby got out. Alice moved up behind the wheel while Laney got into the front passenger seat.

"Once we know something," Toby said to Alice, "I'll call and let you know what to do." He patted his cell phone in his jean pocket.

"You be careful," Alice said.

"We will." Toby gave Alice a peck on the lips.

Laney stuck her head out the window and gazed up at Allen. "Be safe. Love you."

"Love you." Allen turned and the two crept into the trees.

Walking through the tall eucalyptuses, Allen paused and rested his hand on a smooth trunk.

"What are you doing?" Toby asked.

"Having a moment."

"Don't tell me you're talking to that tree."

"Did you know there was a fire here?"

"Huh? When?"

"Twenty years ago."

"It actually told you this?"

"Spoken like a true survivor." Allen gave Toby a wink.

They continued on and soon reached the cyclone fence.

"It's that one over there," Toby said, pointing to one of the vans. He looked up at the tall chain-link fence. "I don't think I can climb that."

"You won't have to. Let's find the gate."

Allen and Toby kept to the shadows and crept along the fence line. The backside of the building was mostly dark with only a single spotlight shining on a loading dock.

When they found the gate, Toby blurted, "Damn, it's locked."

"No problem. Ever pick a lock?" Allen asked.

Toby figured he better not admit to his transgressions when he was a young man.

He watched Allen inspect the bottom of the padlock slot where the key inserted.

Tiny tendrils grew out of Allen's forefinger and slithered through the key slot into the tumblers of the locking mechanism.

Seconds later, the shank released from the locking bar and popped out of the padlock body.

"How'd you learn to do that?" Toby asked.

"You'd be surprised what you can do when you put your mind to it." Allen opened the gate wide enough for them to slip through. They went to the rear of the closest van and kept to the fence as they proceeded down the rear of the vehicles.

"This is it," Toby confirmed, spotting the license plate.

Allen picked the lock on the rear door.

Toby heard a click. Allen turned down the handle and opened the door.

The cargo hold was empty.

Suddenly, spotlights began to pop on casting bright light everywhere as a siren blared.

* * *

Laney saw a bright glow appear on the other side of the trees accompanied by a shrieking alarm.

"Uh-oh," Alice said.

"We better go."

"We can't just leave them."

"Allen won't let anything happen to Toby. Hurry, before somebody comes."

Alice started up the Corolla and pulled away from the curb.

* * *

A back door banged open and six men stormed out of the building. They were uniformly dressed with dark trousers and WE logos on their black shirts.

"This isn't good," Toby said. "What are we going to do?"

"Follow me." Allen scurried toward the end of the parked vans. He slipped around the side of the last vehicle and peeked out from behind the front bumper.

The men split up and canvassed the area.

Allen glanced around for an escape route. He knew he could scale the fence with no problem but doubted if Toby would be able to. They were pinned in with nowhere to go. He noticed the edge of the parking lot overgrown with weeds, the side of the building covered with ivy halfway up the concrete wall, ten feet high.

"Come on!" Allen said and they bolted across the asphalt.

"Hey, you! Stop!" a man yelled.

"There's no way they can get away," another man shouted.

Heavy footsteps charged across the parking lot.

The men converged on the side of the building.

"Where did they go?"

The men looked around with confused expressions on their faces.

"Check the fence. Maybe they crawled under." They split up and went back to the parked vans.

Fifteen minutes later, the men gave up their search and went back into the building. The spotlights and the security alarm eventually turned off.

"Are they gone?" Toby asked, unable to see through the thick foliage.

"I think we're okay." Allen stepped away from the wall. He looked like he was wearing a ghillie suit covered with ivy that a sniper might wear as camouflage. Toby had been standing directly behind him flat against the wall, undetected by the security guards.

"That was pretty slick," Toby said, watching Allen transform his body to the bark-like armor. "So what do we do now?"

"We need to get inside."

"You saw all those guards. There's no way we're getting in there."

"Oh, there is."

"You have a plan?"

"Yeah. But first we need to go to the car."

Toby followed Allen back the way they had come. When they reached the gate, Allen discovered that someone had relocked the padlock. It took him a couple of seconds to reopen it. He pushed the gate wide enough for Toby to squeeze through.

Allen remained where he stood.

He closed the gate and relocked the padlock.

"What are you doing?" Toby asked, gripping the metal mesh and staring through the cyclone fence at Allen who did not respond as he had already turned away and was heading for the rear door that led into the building.

21

DEAD END

"I don't like you being out there all alone," Nora said.

"I'll be fine," Jack said. "Abe will relieve me just after midnight. This might be our only chance of catching these guys."

"True. They're most likely dumping the carcasses at night." Nora poured hot coffee into an insulated tumbler. She put the empty pot on the stove. She twisted on the stopper and snapped on the drinking cup.

Nora handed the flask to Jack.

"Thanks."

"Sure, you don't want me to come along?"

"I'm sure. Besides, I'd appreciate if you'd keep an eye on Lennie. Miguel and I did some major repairs to the barn. I'd hate to see the lummox mess things up."

"You act like he's a bull in a china shop."

"More like a Yeren in a glass house."

"Sometimes I think you're too hard on him."

"Just see he doesn't get into any more trouble."

"Sure thing, Daddy-O."

"Stop that," Jack said, trying his best to suppress a grin.

After kissing Nora goodbye, Jack went outside, jumped into the Ford Expedition, and headed down to the main highway.

He drove for twenty minutes before spotting Miguel's truck parked on the shoulder next to a stand of trees near the junction to the abandoned farmhouse.

Jack pulled up alongside and lowered the passenger window. "Anything?"

"Nope, not yet," Miguel replied from his truck. "Care for some lukewarm coffee?" Miguel held up his travel mug.

"No, thanks. Brought my own."

"Okay then. See you tomorrow."

"Say hi to Maria and Sophia."

"Will do." Miguel started up his truck and drove away.

Jack pulled in between the trees and shut off his engine. He raised the passenger window and lowered the driver's side. A cool breeze chilled his face.

Between the cold air and the hot coffee, he figured he should be able to make it through his watch without falling asleep.

Without anything to do but stare out at the road, boredom soon set in and Jack drifted off sometime before eleven.

He was having a weird dream; he took Lennie to his first day of preschool and was having a difficult time convincing the teacher to let the twelve-foot tall Yeren play with the other children, when the sound of a passing car woke him up. He spotted the dim taillights of a white van racing down the road.

Jack started up the Expedition. The SUV peeled out like a State Trooper cruiser coming out from behind a speed trap concealment. He continued to accelerate, losing the vehicle on the windy road.

He caught sight of the taillights again, matching his speed with the van up ahead, pulling back when he feared he was too close so as not to tip the driver that he was being followed.

Jack stayed razor-sharp, maneuvering the treacherous road with its unexpected sharp bends. A few times the van would slow down and Jack had to decelerate fast. At one point he switched off his low beams and turned on his fog lights, hoping the driver wouldn't see Jack's headlights in his side mirrors.

After more than an hour, the van's taillights brightened as the vehicle turned off the road.

Jack slowed down, passing a road marker: CB-17. He saw the entrance to a dirt road stretching into the trees. He pulled off onto the shoulder and shut off the engine.

He gazed through the passenger window and saw slivers of red glowing between the trees.

And then the taillights vanished.

Jack grabbed his cell phone out of the cup holder. He checked for a signal. Not only was it strong, he had four bars of battery life. He snatched a flashlight from the glove compartment and got out of the Expedition.

A slight breeze rustled the pines. Somewhere in the trees, an owl gave a familiar hoot. He heard what sounded like a hinge grinding in the distance.

He hiked up the dark road, keeping the beam of the flashlight on the ground just ahead of him. After covering maybe a hundred yards, he came to a closed gate.

He walked up to the gate, hoping it was only latched. Instead he found it had an electronic box and could only be opened by remote control. He stood up on the railing and climbed over the gate.

It was pitch dark under the canopy. He scanned the surrounding branches, looking for surveillance cameras. If there were any, he couldn't see them.

Jack followed the beam of his flashlight.

The road up ahead seemed to come to an abrupt dead end.

"Where'd you go?" Jack muttered, shining his flashlight on the tree trunks as he walked toward them. He could see the ground gradually slope down.

Jack took his cell phone out of his pocket, placed it next to the base of a tree, and covered it with pine needles.

He started down the incline and entered the mouth of the underground tunnel.

22

DULLES

Nick leaned in front of Meg so he could gaze out the oval-shaped window. "Oh my God, the entire runway's on fire." Even though it was after three in the morning Eastern Standard Time and the sky was blanketed with dark clouds, the airport 2,000 feet below was brightly lit up and looked like it was being besieged by a firestorm.

Miniature-sized emergency vehicles rushed to the fractured fuselage of the commercial airliner as fire trucks battled the blaze. Fiery wreckage was strewn for a quarter mile.

Shadowy silhouettes circled over the carnage like black demons.

The pilot's voice spoke over the address system, "Ladies and gentlemen, we will no longer be able to land at Ronald Reagan Washington National Airport. Ground control has diverted us to Dulles. We apologize for the inconvenience and should be touching down in twenty minutes."

Nick flinched when a winged shape swept over the wing. "Jesus, did you see that? It's a wonder it didn't get sucked up into the engine."

Meg clutched his hand and shut her eyes. "Tell me when we're safe on the ground. Talk about a nightmare."

Nick didn't know if she was referring to the burning plane down on the tarmac or the ordeal dealing with their delayed flight, having to disembark the plane while the two bodies were removed, then having to wait an additional two hours while Animal Control captured the poisonous flying snake so janitorial services could disinfect the passenger compartment. "You'll feel better once we're at our hotel."

"And we've hit the bar," Meg said.

Nick checked his watch, which had already changed to the new time zone. "I doubt if the cocktail lounge will be open."

"Then there better be a wet bar in the room."

"Or we can get room service."

* * *

Nick was attempting to lift the heavy suitcase from the revolving turnstile at baggage claim when a man and woman approached; both dressed in black business suits.

"Mr. Wells?" the man asked.

"Yes, I'm Nick Wells."

"I'm FBI Special Agent Mack Hunter." He motioned to his partner. "And this is Special Agent Anna Rivers."

"You must be Meg Wells," Anna said.

"That's right," Meg replied.

"What is this all about? Have we done something wrong?" Nick asked.

"No, not at all," Mack said. "We're here to make sure you have a safe stay."

"Are we in some kind of danger?"

"We're just taking precautions," Anna said.

"Against what?" Meg asked.

"There have been some threats made by an organization that calls themselves Cryptos."

"You mean like a street gang?" Nick asked.

"No, nothing like that. They're a radical group that wants to protect the cryptids."

"That's absurd," Meg growled. "Who in their right mind would want to do that?"

"Like I said, they're a bunch of extremists."

"So, what do these...Cryptos...look like?" Nick asked.

"They're easy to spot," Mack said. "Dark clothes, hoodies, animal masks. Most carry concealed weapons."

"And you think they might come after us?" Nick asked.

"It's public knowledge that Nick will be testifying in front of Senator Rollins's oversight committee," Mack said.

"It's best we take precautions," Anna assured Nick. "The senator has also been a target."

Meg smiled at the two agents. "Well, I have no objection." She looked at Nick who was still trying to wrestle their heavy suitcase off the carousel. "Honey?"

"Fine by me. Agent Hunter. Could you give me a hand? It seems to be caught on something."

"Sure." Mack grabbed the handle and hoisted the travel bag effortlessly off the carousel and onto the floor like it was light as air.

"Uh, thanks," Nick said, feeling a little stupid but then thankful they were in competent hands.

23

THERMAL TREATMENT

Allen breached the building's security system and made his way inside. He felt bad for tricking Toby, but he knew it would be too dangerous for his friend to accompany him after seeing the large number of security guards that had come out to investigate the perimeter of the building when the alarm had sounded.

Being that it was after hours and no one was working, Allen was puzzled why there were so many guards on duty.

Most of the overhead fluorescent lights had been turned off with only a few left on so the corridors would not be completely pitch black.

Allen crept along the walls, darkening the leafy mosaic of his epidermis into a blackish fungal spore so he could blend in with the shadows and hopefully avoid being detected by the surveillance cameras positioned in the hallways.

The lower floor was a maze of business office cubicles and glass-partitioned pharmaceutical assembly lines.

None of which triggered his pheromone senses.

Allen heard voices and advanced warily down the hall. He took a quick peek around a doorframe and saw five men sitting in a break room.

Three were playing a game of cards at a table, while the other two men occupied a couch, one reading a magazine, the other staring at his cell phone.

Allen stepped back and turned down a corridor where the hallway intersected.

A door swung open and a guard stepped out of the men's room. "Jesus, what the—" but before the man could finish, Allen balled his hand into a fist and flicked out his fingers, releasing a purplish cloud of pollen into the man's face.

The guard inhaled a lungful of lavender dust, which rapidly dropped his heart rate. He gasped and instantly fell into a deep sleep. Allen caught him before he hit the floor. He dragged the unconscious man back into the restroom.

Allen came out into the hall and felt a tingling sensation.

The scent was getting stronger.

A thick gauge metal door was at the end of a narrow hall. Allen went up to the door and found it unlocked.

He pushed open the door, reached in, and flicked the wall switch.

Cinderblock walls enclosed the forty-foot square room. A fifteen-foot long conveyor belt suspended three feet off the floor ended at a metal housing the size of a large SUV, which had a stack on the top of the unit that rose up to the ceiling.

Allen saw half a dozen flat carts parked against a wall. He spotted a split-open olive green parcel left on a cart.

A control box with various buttons and switches was on a post next to the conveyor belt. Allen pushed a red button.

The front door made a racket as it hoisted upward.

"You sons of bitches!" Allen yelled when he saw the ash remains in the incinerator.

"Told you he'd be pissed," a voice said behind him.

Allen spun around.

The five security guards he had seen taking a break stood just inside the room. He hadn't heard them come in because of the noisy incinerator door.

Allen knew he didn't have to worry about the man in the restroom; he'd be in dreamland for the next hour.

"What's with the getup?" the tall, skinny guard said who looked to be in charge as he was the only one wearing a sidearm.

"Yeah, it's not Halloween," joked another guard. He slapped a steel expandable baton across his palm.

Allen could feel his inner core heating up as his rage fumed. His outer epidermis was no longer covered with dark-brown fungal spores and had changed into a waxy red shell. He glared at the other three men who were wielding similar batons. "You guys are making a big mistake."

"Well, what do you know: it speaks," taunted the tall, skinny guard.

"No buddy, you made the mistake coming in here." A chubby guard raised his baton and charged Allen.

Instead of retreating, Allen ran at the man. Allen blocked the downward swing with one arm and grabbed the man's face. Capsaicinoids secreted from Allen's palm onto the man's face, his scream muffled as the chemical compounds burned his skin and oozed into his mouth and down his throat like liquid fire.

The metal club clanked on the concrete as the man fell to the floor.

"What the hell?" The tall, skinny guard drew his sidearm. He cocked his weapon, aimed, and fired a single shot.

The bullet punched a hole in Allen's chest and came out his back, ricocheting off the steel incinerator and chipping a piece of cinderblock out of the wall.

"Perhaps you'd like a taste." Allen lunged at the tall, skinny man. He knocked the gun from his hand and swiped his fingers across the man's mouth. The guard's eyes grew wide with tears and his face reddened. His metabolism went berserk causing mucus to flow from his nostrils like a spigot and his pores to perspire profusely. He passed out in a puddle of his own sweat.

Allen grabbed a guard by the arm and swung him against the cinderblock, knocking him out.

A guard threw down his baton and bolted out of the room.

The last guard, the biggest of the lot, wasn't deterred and rushed Allen. They crashed into the conveyor belt. The big man punched Allen in the face, which had little effect but was enough of a jolt he fell back onto the rubber runner.

The guard reached up and punched some buttons on the control panel.

Inside the incinerator, rows of flames shot out of the sidewalls.

"So long, pal," the guard said, watching Allen being transported toward the inferno as the conveyor belt began to move.

"Perhaps you would like to join me." Allen reached up, grabbed the man by the front of the shirt, and pulled him down onto the moving conveyor belt.

"Hey, what the hell are you doing? Let go of me!"

"Not until you tell me who put you up to this."

"I'm not telling you shit." The guard tried to roll off the conveyor belt but Allen held on with a firm grip. The man gawked at the incinerator, his face aglow from the bright blaze. "Come on, man. This isn't funny. Let me go!"

"Who's your boss?" Allen could feel the radiating heat. He caught a glimpse of a temperature gauge. The interior of the incinerator had already reached 1400 degrees.

The man's shirt was soaked from his sweat. He pushed his arms up hoping to break free from Allen's strong grip. Allen tucked his legs into his belly, swung out from under the big man, and slipped onto the floor.

When the man tried to get off the conveyor belt, he found that his hands were stuck in a sticky substance left on the rubber mat by Allen.

"This is your last chance," Allen said, getting to his feet. The man was only a foot away from entering the flaming gas jets, crisscrossing like overlapping fingers of fire.

"Stop this thing! Jesus, will you...okay, okay, I'll tell you!"

"Better talk fast."
The man screamed out a name.
Allen punched a button and the conveyor belt stopped.

24

THE LAIR

Automatic sensors triggered the tunnel lights the moment Jack reached level ground. He rushed over to the wall, switched off his flashlight, and remained still.

Seconds later the cavern was pitched into darkness. He raised his right arm to test the motion detectors. The lights remained off.

Judging by the immense size of the tunnel, he figured it was meant for vehicles and not foot traffic as the sensors seemed to be directed at the center of the roadway, not on the concave walls.

Jack felt his way along the wall and continued further into the tunnel. It wasn't long before he spotted a single dome light on the ceiling shining down over a garage area with vans and trucks.

He crept over to the side of a van and peeked around the front of the vehicle. He could see a metal door in the concrete wall. A security camera was positioned above the door. He had no doubt there was someone sitting inside a control room keeping an eye on the vehicles on a surveillance monitor.

The overhead lights came on as a loud engine rumbled down the tunnel. Jack crouched behind the front tire.

A black Rolls-Royce Cullinan pulled up to the entry door. Jack remembered reading a *Motor Trend* magazine stating that it was the most expensive utility vehicle in the world with an outrageous manufactured list price of $325,000.

Two bodyguards got out from the front, brandishing Uzi pistols with long extended ammunition clips. Each man stood over six feet tall, his bulging muscles ready to rip out of his business suit like the Incredible Hulk.

A bodyguard opened the rear passenger door.

Lucas Finder, COO of Wilde Enterprises stepped out.

And then Carter Wilde exited the exorbitant SUV.

He looked more like an aging movie star than a billionaire businessman with his full beard and his gray hair pulled back in a tight ponytail. He wore a long, black cassock and black boots.

Attired in his clerical garb, Wilde seemed protected in a saintly aura.

Jack heard locking bolts disengage as the entry door opened slowly.

A bodyguard waited until the door was open all the way then proceeded inside, followed by Wilde, then Finder, with the other big man taking up the rear.

The heavy metal door swung slowly, rigged with a self closer.

Jack scurried out from behind the van and managed to slip between the edge of the bone-crushing door and the doorjamb with an inch to spare. He stayed close to the wall as the door sealed shut.

The four men reached a junction in the hall and turned down an adjacent corridor.

He could feel the vibration of machines humming as forced air and liquids surged through overhead pipes.

Farther away in the bowels of the subterranean place, pitiful whimpering that sounded almost human mingled with growls of animalistic rage.

Coming to a bank of windows, Jack snuck a peek into what appeared to be a dimly lit laboratory. He didn't see anyone working inside, so he kept going down the hall, not bothering to duck down.

When he arrived at the junction, he decided to turn left to avoid Wilde and his entourage. Even though he was wearing his holstered Colt .44 Magnum revolver, Jack knew he would be outgunned going up against the bodyguards' submachine guns.

The dimly lit corridor stretched for more than fifty feet and the right hand wall soon became a string of ceiling-high steel bars.

Jack strained his eyes to see inside the cage. It was black as a bottomless pit. He pointed his flashlight between the bars and switched it on.

A dozen creatures squawked and charged the bars, causing Jack to jump back.

The turkey-sized dinosaurs had short black manes and beaks with tiny teeth. Their bodies were covered with blue plumes and had flaming-red feathered wings with clawed fingers. They had long bare legs, talon feet, and flared feathered tails.

Jack recalled seeing such specimens on one of Nora's cryptozoology charts.

The bird-like dinosaurs were *Caudipteryx*, thought to have lived in the Aptian age of the early Cretaceous period in China.

The damn things were making enough noise to wake the dead.

"Quiet! Shut up!" Jack snapped, switching off his flashlight, hoping that would silence the creatures. They kept squawking like their heads were about to be placed on the chopping block.

Suddenly, Jack heard footsteps and a bright beam of light shined in his face.

"Well, well. Who do we have here?"

Jack shielded his eyes. He knew that voice without seeing the man's face. "So this is where you've been hiding?"

"And now you've found me."

Jack let his hand slide down by the butt of his gun.

"Uh, uh. I wouldn't do that."

The overhead lights came on.

A man with a shaggy gray beard, wearing a white lab coat flecked with blood, stood with Carter Wilde, Lucas Finder, and the two bodyguards, who at the moment had their Uzi pistols trained on Jack.

"It's so nice of you to join us, Jack."

"Too bad I can't say the same, McCabe."

"Still upset about the prison thing, I see."

"Can you shut those things up?" Wilde said to McCabe.

"Sure thing, Carter." The doctor reached in his lab pocket and took out an electronic tablet. He tapped the screen a few times.

Jack heard a series of *snapping* sounds and the small dinosaurs stopped their raucous noise. That's when he noticed they were all wearing tight collars around their small necks. Dr. McCabe was controlling their behavior with shock therapy.

"Thank you," Wilde said. He looked at Jack. "So, how did you get here?"

"Followed one of your vans."

Wilde turned to one of his bodyguards. "I'm sure he didn't come here on foot. Round up some men and go find his vehicle."

The burly man turned and marched down the hall.

"We know about the dumping site," Jack said.

Wilde glared at Dr. McCabe. "What's he talking about?"

"We've had a few hiccups. Nothing for you to worry about."

"Don't give me that, Joel," Wilde snapped. "Don't forget who's running this show."

It was the first time Jack had ever seen Carter Wilde and Dr. Joel McCabe together.

He couldn't help noticing similarities between the two men.

Maybe it was the beards and the fact they were the same height and build.

There was the contrast between the billionaire dressed in black and the geneticist in his white lab coat—like ebony and ivory.

Yin and Yang.

Or in their case: oil and water.

Two opposing forces seemingly joined for a singular purpose.

Jack couldn't help wondering if it was even remotely possible the two men might be related.

And if so, why had Wilde and McCabe been keeping it a secret for all these years?

25

MILITARY MAP

When Abe had gone to relieve Jack, he was surprised to see Jack's Expedition gone.

After driving around the back roads to see if Jack had decided to park somewhere else, and not finding him, Abe went back to the road junction figuring Jack must have gone home just before midnight and had nothing to report.

Abe attempted contacting Jack on his cell phone to check up on him. Jack didn't pick up so he had to leave a message on Jack's voicemail.

For some reason, something didn't seem right.

Call it sheriff's intuition.

Which is why Abe called Nora at the house just before sunup and learned that Jack had never come home.

Abe was bone-weary from staying up all night. He nuked a mug of hot water in the office microwave oven and stirred in some instant coffee crystals. It was a far cry from Clare's delicious dark roasted brew and was only somewhat palatable when he added some powdered creamer and a couple of packets of artificial sweetener.

Abe heard a truck pull up in the parking lot out front.

A few seconds later, the glass door opened, and Nora and Miguel entered.

"Anything?" Abe asked.

"No," Nora said. "I've been trying his cell phone, but he doesn't pick up."

"It's not like him not to answer his phone," Miguel said.

"I thought it was odd that he didn't wait around for me," Abe admitted. "I'm going to put out an APB with the highway patrol."

"Before you do that, I have a better idea. Jack has a location tracker on his phone. I have the app on my computer." Nora put her laptop on the counter. It took a moment to boot up. She positioned the laptop so Abe and Miguel could see the screen.

A red dot was in the middle of the online map with the latitude and longitude of Jack's exact location in the right hand portion of the screen.

"That's out in the middle of nowhere," Miguel said. "Nothing but forest."

"Let me check those GPS coordinates with something I have." Abe stepped over to a filing cabinet. He opened the second drawer, flipped through the dividers, and pulled out a folded map. He shut the drawer and spread the map out on the counter.

"What's that?" Miguel asked.

"An old friend of mine used to be a cartographer in the Army. He liked to collect old military maps. When he died, he wanted me to have them. Kind of a remembrance I suppose."

"He was a mapmaker?" Miguel asked.

"That's right."

Nora gazed at the map on her screen then compared the grids with the topographic paper version. She tapped her forefinger on a spot with black rectangular shapes. "What's this?"

Abe leaned in for a closer look. He flipped a portion of the map over so he could read the legend on the back. "That used to be an underground missile site during World War II. Nike's I believe. Has some aboveground barracks and such. Says here it was closed down in 1956. Wonder what Jack was doing around there?"

"Maybe he stopped to take a leak and dropped his phone."

"I doubt that, Miguel." Nora looked at Abe. "How big do you think this place is?"

"Judging by the scale at the bottom of the page, I'd say it's probably the size of a shopping mall."

Abe saw Nora's eyes grow wide. "What if this is McCabe's secret lab?"

"So why didn't Jack call and let us know?" Miguel asked.

"Maybe he doesn't have his phone. Someone might have taken it."

"Miguel and I will go look for him," Abe said. "On the way maybe I can get a couple deputies from the next county to tag along."

"What about me?" Nora said.

"I'd like it if you could stay here," Abe said. "In case he shows up. Could you also check on Clare? I hate thinking of her out there alone."

"Sure Abe, I can do that."

"Don't worry," Abe said. "We'll find him."

26

ROOM SERVICE

"How'd you sleep?" Nick asked, turning onto his side so he could look at Meg.

She lowered the covers from her chin, smiled, and ran the edge of the top sheet between her thumb and forefinger. "Is this silk? Feels like 1800 thread. We really should get us a set."

"Don't forget we're staying at a five-star hotel, courtesy of the United States government. I doubt we could afford it."

Meg got cozy under the covers. "How about we spend the day in bed?"

"Sure, I guess I could blow off the congressional hearing."

"Tell them you have a sore throat and can't testify."

"Yeah, like that would fly." Nick sat up and swung his feet onto the carpet. He kneaded his toes into the plush pile like John McClane in *Die Hard* then got up and walked over to the small table by a leather chair. He picked up a remote control and opened the drapes, revealing a breathtaking view from the high-rise window.

Nick sat in the chair and grabbed his cell phone off the table. "I have a text from Special Agent Hunter. They'll swing by our room in an hour and escort us to the hearing."

"What about breakfast?"

"Yeah, that doesn't give us much time. I'll call down for room service while we're getting ready." Nick walked over to the nightstand. He picked up the suite phone and was about to call the front desk when someone knocked on the door.

Meg sat up in bed. "Who could that be?"

Nick went to the door and looked out the peephole. "It's room service with a cart."

"But you didn't call."

"Hunter must have arranged it."

"Strange he never mentioned it in his text."

"Think I should give him a call?" Nick glanced through the peephole again. "The waiter looks normal enough."

"Let him in. If I don't eat something soon I think I'm going to be sick."

Nick turned the security deadbolt and opened the door.

"Good morning, sir." The man was in his early twenties and wore a hotel uniform.

"Morning. Please, come in," Nick said and held the door open so the man could push the serving cart into the room.

"Shall I set you up at the table by the window?" the waiter asked.

"Yes, that would be perfect," Nick replied.

Meg waited until the waiter's back was turned then quickly climbed out of bed and slipped into the hotel robe lying on the foot of the bed.

"Are you enjoying your stay?" the waiter asked. He set two plates on the table with cloth napkins and cutlery.

"So far," Nick replied. It was hard to give an honest answer as the only thing they had done since arriving was sleep.

"Any big plans for today?"

"Well, I'm supposed to..." but then Nick decided he better not divulge too much to a stranger. "We're just going to take in the sights. Lincoln's Memorial, the Washington Monument, that sort of thing."

The waiter placed a large covered silver-serving tray in the middle of the table.

Nick had no idea if a tip had been included in the meal and thought he should give the young man something for his services. He went over to his side of the bed to retrieve his wallet from the nightstand.

"So I gather you won't be attending Rollins's dog and pony show?"

"Nick?" Meg took a step back and self-consciously tightened the sash on her robe.

Nick turned around.

The waiter smiled and reached under the cloth draped on the side of the cart.

Nick heard a click then the suite door flew open.

"Drop it!" yelled Special Agent Hunter. He had his Glock aimed directly at the waiter. "Hands where I can see them!"

The young man put his hands in the air.

Special Agent Rivers burst into the room. She stepped behind the man, drew one arm back, and then the other, and cinched his wrists with a zip tie. She pushed him into the chair by the window.

"What'd he have?" Hunter asked.

Rivers reached under the cloth draped on the side of the cart. She came up with a .22 caliber pistol that looked like it might be used for target practice at a gun range. "So what where you planning to do with this?" she asked the young man in the chair.

"I was just going to scare them, that's all."

Rivers pushed the release button and the clip fell out of the handgrip onto the floor. She cocked the slide back and ejected the round still in the chamber. "So why don't I believe you?"

"Who is he?" Nick asked.

"There's something I neglected to mention." Rivers spread the man's shirt apart, popping the buttons. She pulled back the neck of his shirt to expose the tattoo on his left shoulder.

A large black C in an archaic font style was superimposed over four red slashes, the tattoo looking as though the man's arm had been savagely clawed by a wild animal.

"They all have them."

"You don't think he was really going to hurt us?" Meg asked.

"Don't let that innocent face fool you," Hunter said.

The young man locked eyes on Meg for a moment, then looked at Nick and gave him a snide grin.

It gave Nick the chills.

27

GOAT DROPPINGS

"Shouldn't you be notifying the State Police?' Clare asked, rustling up some food for Abe and Miguel to take along. She saw Miguel through the kitchen window, waiting for the sheriff in the front passenger seat of the Bronco.

"I will when I know more," Abe said. "No point in calling in the troops and finding out Jack just lost his phone and ends up showing up out of the blue."

"You really believe that?"

Abe shook his head and placed his Steven Model 69RXL pump shotgun on the kitchen table. Clare knew he liked the weapon because it was lightweight and suited for police work. She figured he'd let Miguel use it and keep the Remington pump mounted in the Bronco for himself.

"Did you remember to stock up on .12 gauge shells?" Abe asked.

"Gun cabinet, bottom drawer," Clare said.

Abe went out into the living room.

Clare heard him unlock the glass doors and rummage through the drawers. He came back into the kitchen and tossed the ammunition boxes into a small equipment bag along with his 9mm Beretta. He zipped up the bag, slung the strap over his shoulder, and grabbed the riot gun.

Clare followed Abe out the back door, carrying the cooler of food and drinks.

Rounder bounded across the yard to greet them while Abe lowered the rear window of the Bronco and placed the shotgun and gear bag behind the rear seat. He took the cooler from Clare, placed it inside, and closed the window.

"You be careful," Clare said.

"Don't worry. You know me. Can't stay away too long or I'll be missing your home cooking."

"Is that all you'll be missing?"

Abe leaned down and kissed her tenderly on the lips. "What do you think?"

"The sooner you're gone, the sooner you'll be back."

"Sounds like something Yogi Berra would say."

"You know what I mean," Clare said and gave him a playful punch in the arm before he climbed into the Bronco.

She gave Miguel a wave and watched them pull around and head down the long gravel driveway.

Rounder sat by her feet. He stared at the truck as it turned onto the main road and disappeared behind the trees. The dog swiveled its head and looked up at Clare.

"Don't worry, boy. He'll be back before you know it."

Rounder let out a loud bark then bolted across the yard.

"Where're you off to?"

The Pyrenean Mountain Dog came to a crashing halt, spun around to look at Clare, and barked again.

"What?"

Rounder charged into the tall grass behind the pens where some of the goats were inside eating feed from the trough.

"All right. I'm coming." Clare trudged after Rounder. She watched the big dog racing through the grass. Finally, he stopped and gave her an impatient bark.

"Hold your horses." Clare walked up to Rounder. He was sniffing a few scraps of wood.

"How the hell did this get all the way out here?" A board was cracked and another snapped in two. She thought she could salvage most of it and rebuild the milking stand.

Rounder cocked his head skyward and jumped up on Clare, knocking her to the ground.

"What has gotten into—?"

An object plummeted to the ground, landing five feet away.

Clare stared at the mangled goat embedded in the blood-splattered dirt. She rose to her feet and drew the Ruger revolver from her holster.

A dark shadow loomed over her. She looked up expecting to see a passing cloud. All she saw was a soaring shape blocking out the sun.

Another goat struck the ground.

Shielding her eyes from the bright sunshine, Clare stared skyward and walked backwards through the grass. Rounder was jumping up and down, barking at the winged creatures circling above.

Clare counted six flying overhead. "Rounder, come!" She spun around and raced for the goat pens.

A raven-black Thunderbird grabbed a goat by the scruff with its sharp talons. The raptor flapped its twenty-foot wide wings and hoisted the goat off the ground.

On the run, Clare took aim and fired off a single shot.

The bullet struck the giant bird in the head. It folded its wings, releasing the goat before it crashed to the ground. The goat landed on its feet and ran across the pen to the other goats huddled against the fence.

A Thunderbird swooped down to grab Rounder.

Clare ran at the attacker with her gun hand extended. She fired two rounds over Rounder's head and into the predator's chest. Rounder sidestepped the falling bird before it fell on top of him.

Clare's jacket was snared from behind and she was hoisted off her feet. She gazed down at her boots and saw the ground pulling away. She had an aerial view of the top of the goat shed, then the peaked roof of her house, and the pyramid tops of the surrounding trees as the mighty Thunderbird circled the property.

Sharp talons dug through her jacket and into her flesh.

She spotted another raptor high in the sky release a captured goat to fall to its death. A typical killing method used by Thunderbirds. After their prey struck the ground, the tenderized meat would be easier to consume.

Still holding her gun, Clare reached back with her free hand and grabbed the bottom of the bird's leg. The skin was rough and scaly.

She looked down, estimating she was over a hundred feet in the air—a death-drop for sure.

A Thunderbird soared below her as though the two birds were flying in formation.

They were about to glide over the steel roof of the goat shed. This would be her only chance.

Clare aimed down past her right boot and shot the giant raptor under her in the back of the neck to sever the spine. She then raised her arm, firing her two remaining bullets into the underbelly of her capturer, hoping for a crippling shot to the heart.

She shoved her gun back into its holster and grabbed hold of the bird's leg with both hands as she and the two birds went spiraling down.

28

CATCH OF THE DAY

Allen entered the cottage and found Laney sitting in the front room with Toby and Alice. Laney jumped out of her chair and dashed over to Allen, wrapping her arms around his neck. "Honey, we were so worried."

Toby rose from the couch. "What happened in there? We waited but you never came out so we came back here."

After giving Laney a hug, Allen eased out of her embrace. He went over to the couch and slumped down next to Alice.

"Allen? What's wrong? You look terrible," Alice said, commenting on his ragged appearance from his rough brawl with the security guards.

"It's all gone," Allen muttered. "Every last bag."

"Gone where?" Laney asked.

"The damn fools burned it."

Toby grabbed his thin gray hair with both hands like he was going to rip it out and collapsed in the chair Laney had been sitting in. "That's crazy. Do they have any idea what they've done?"

"It's not the end of the world," Laney said, kneeling next to the couch to console Allen. "We've had setbacks before."

Allen lowered his head and stared at their interlocking fingers. "Six months worth of work up in smoke."

"Laney's right," Alice pitched in. "Next time we'll be more careful."

"Right now, all I want to do is decompress," Allen said, feeling deflated from the tragic loss, the thousands of people with life-threatening illnesses who could have been treated with the remedy destroyed in the incinerator.

He glanced at the coffee table and spotted an envelope lying on top of an issue of *Garden Culture Magazine*. He leaned forward, retrieved the correspondence, and stared at the return address. "It's from the FDA."

"Open it up," Alice said.

Laney let go of Allen's hand.

The tip of Allen's forefinger became razor sharp and made the ideal letter opener.

He sliced through the top of the envelope, took out the folded letter, and opened it up. He read a few lines then crumpled it up, and threw the ball of paper on the floor.

"Allen, what's wrong?" Laney said, picking up the wadded-up letter.

"We've been rejected."

"How can that be?" Alice asked. "Your plants work. We're living examples. Surely their tests can confirm that!"

"Hey, we'll fight this thing. Maybe there was a screw up on their end," Toby said.

Laney flattened out the letter on the coffee table and read through it. "Or maybe this letter is bogus."

Allen looked over at Laney. "What do you mean?"

"I don't think it came from the FDA. There's no evaluation or real reason stated here for the rejection. I would think there would be test results from the CDER at least."

"What's the CDER?" Toby asked.

"It's the Center for Drug Evaluation and Research. They're the one's that do the actual testing for the FDA."

"Let me see." Allen moved off the couch and sat next to Laney. He gave the letter a second read. "That's not all. Check out the letterhead. Since when does Wilde Enterprises have ties with the FDA?"

Laney shrugged. "Think the address is legitimate?'

"Only one way to find out," Allen said. "Anyone up for a road trip?"

Alice glanced down at the return address on the envelope. "In my car?"

"I was thinking we might take the Barracuda."

"What, you know where it is?" Toby asked, astonished.

"Not at the moment, but I can find it," Allen assured his friend.

* * *

"You can let us out here," Allen said, sitting in the backseat of the taxi with Toby.

Allen wore an old jogging outfit of Toby's and had the hood up on the sweatshirt so the driver couldn't see his face.

"You sure? This looks like a pretty rough neighborhood," the driver said, waving his hand at the rundown apartment buildings and the gloomy back alleys; warehouses on each side of the street that looked abandoned and destined for the wrecking ball.

Toby glanced at the meter, pulled some money out of his wallet, and handed the bills to the driver. "Keep the change. There's a little extra for freezing you out."

"Thanks. Sure this is the place?"

"I'm sure," Allen told the driver.

Allen and Toby opened their doors and got out. The taxi driver made a U-turn and sped off down the street like he was in a big hurry to go somewhere else.

"Where to now?" Toby asked.

Using his acute senses, Allen had been able to detect the pheromone lingering in the air left by the residue in the trunk of Toby's Barracuda, which was why he had insisted the taxi's windows be down even though the ride over had been rather chilly. He knew the car thieves had driven this street, as the scent was getting increasingly stronger.

He stepped off the curb. "This way." Toby followed him across the street. They turned down a breezeway between two five-story buildings and entered a back alley cluttered with over-filled garbage cans spilling onto the asphalt, discarded junk, soiled mattresses, and old appliances.

A shrill noise screeched from an open doorway fifty feet away.

"That's a torque wrench." Toby balled his bony hands into fists. "Don't tell me it's a chop shop."

They crept over to a roll-up door partially raised off the concrete.

"There's just enough room for me to crawl under." Allen shrugged out of the sweatshirt and then the pants. He kicked off Toby's old sneakers. "I'll call you when I'm through."

"Not on your life," Toby protested.

Allen looked Toby straight in the face. "There's no telling how many are in there. I doubt very seriously if they're going to just hand over your car. Stay here."

Toby was about to argue when the torque wrench went silent.

Allen put his asparagus-looking finger up to his olive-colored lips, cutting Toby off before he could argue any further, then dropped to the ground and rolled under the aluminum door.

The interior looked like a typical auto garage. Two hydraulic lifts were by the back wall. A gray BMW sedan was suspended six feet off the ground. The doors had been removed, along with the hood and the trunk, and all four tires. A dismantled black Jaguar was on the other hoist.

A man in a grimy pair of overalls was standing under the British export. He wore a welder's shield and was in the process of cutting a section of the chassis with an acetylene torch.

Two men were busy inside a new model Cadillac Escalade, removing the dashboard and unbolting the door panels.

The front tires of a Porsche were raised off the ground, held up by a floor jack positioned under the frame. A pair of boots extended out from under the side of the sports car as the man on the creeper underneath disassembled parts of the undercarriage.

Allen crept along the wall and hid behind a stack of tires with matching chrome wheels. He glanced around and saw two other men.

One was loading engine parts onto a cart.

The other man stood in front of a lime-green Plymouth Barracuda—Toby's car.

He reached inside the grill, popped the hood, and took a moment to gawk at the engine. "Hey, Fetcher. Come take a look at this baby."

The man named Fetcher dropped a starter motor onto the cart, wiped his hands on a shop rag, and walked over to the muscle car. He placed his hands on the fender and leaned under the hood to give the engine the once-over. "Been a while since I've seen a V-8 Hemi 440 this cherry. Hell, Bernie, makes you almost hate to have to tear it apart."

"I wouldn't let it worry you too much," Allen said, having crept up behind the two men.

Fetcher spun around first and was met with a hail of blinding pollen, which sent him into an eye-watering sneezing fit. He dropped to his hands and knees, struggling to breathe.

Allen reached up and slammed the hood down on Bernie's head, rendering him unconscious, and hoping the man slumped over the grill of the car wasn't wearing anything that might scratch Toby's prime metallic paintjob.

Knowing he had only seconds to spare, Allen dashed across the garage. He grabbed the long handle of the floor jack and twisted the end. The front end of the Porsche lowered on top of the man lying underneath. Allen made sure he was only pinned on the creeper and not crushed under the vehicle's weight.

"Hey, who the hell's screwing around? Get this thing off me!"

The man's shout alerted the two men stripping the inside of the Cadillac. They jumped out of the SUV and ran at Allen. The man with a wrench swung his tool at Allen's head. Allen ducked to avoid being hit and was immediately grabbed around the midsection from behind by the other man who shouted, "What the hell! This guy feels like a frickin' sponge."

The man with the wrench stared at Allen. "What the hell are you?"

Allen couldn't blame the guy. During the altercation, Allen was transforming himself into defense mode. Even though he remained in his human shape, his outer layer was rapidly changing into an army-green hard shell with...

Projectile spines flew out of Allen.

The man standing in front of Allen dropped to his knees and frantically pulled at the quills lodged in his face.

"Good God!" yelled the man, releasing him from the bear hug as his chest and the insides of his arms were impaled with hundreds of rosebush thorns.

"Not so fast, freak!"

Allen heard the hiss of the acetylene torch and threw up his arm. The steel-cutting flame melted his hand but Allen didn't feel any pain.

"How about we have ourselves a little weenie roast?" growled the welder.

"Let's not." Toby slammed the base of a fire extinguisher canister against the back of the man's skull. The welder fell to the cement. Toby reached down and turned off the nozzle.

"Thanks, Toby."

"Guess I saved your bacon." He looked at the smoldering stump where Allen's hand used to be. "That doesn't look so good."

"Don't worry, it'll grow back."

"We should get out of here."

Allen heard footfalls and men moaning, and then a loud bang as some of the car thieves made their escape out a side door. "I'm all for that."

Toby went over and pushed a button on a control panel. The aluminum roll-up door opened slowly.

Allen raised the Barracuda's hood with one hand, pulled the man out, and closed the hood. He went around to the passenger side and got into the front seat. He glanced under the steering column and saw the bare wires where the carjacker had hotwired the ignition.

Toby got behind the wheel. Instead of using his car keys, he went ahead and touched the loose wires together.

The powerful engine roared like an angry beast inside the garage.

"Thanks for finding my Barracuda," Toby said, steering the muscle car into the alley and stopping.

"No problem," Allen smiled. He opened his door, leaned out, and collected Toby's gym clothes and sneakers off the ground. He sat back in the seat and closed the door. "Quite the catch of the day, wouldn't you say?"

29

KURTZ AND DOBSON

Abe pulled onto the shoulder behind the cruiser parked ten feet from the edge of the two-lane road.

No sooner had Abe shut off the engine, the two sheriff deputies were out of their patrol car and walking toward the front of the Bronco.

"They seem pretty young," Miguel said, watching them through the windshield.

The deputies were in their early twenties, crew cuts, and lean physiques. They looked spit shined and polished like a pair of squeaky-clean recruits straight out of the academy.

"They may look wet behind the ears but they're good officers. They come highly recommended by their boss."

Miguel gave Abe a skeptical look.

"Don't worry. He's a good friend of mine." Abe opened his door and climbed out.

Miguel got out on his side.

"Sheriff Stone, it's a pleasure to meet you. I'm Deputy Frank Kurtz," said the taller officer, holding out his hand.

Abe shook the man's hand. "Deputy Kurtz."

"Sir, I'm Deputy Daniel Dobson," the other officer said.

"Good to meet you," Abe said, shaking Dobson's hand.

Abe turned and introduced Miguel. Again, there was an exchange of handshakes.

"So what's the assignment?" Kurtz asked. "We weren't exactly briefed."

"I'll show you." Abe went back to the Bronco to retrieve the military map. He walked over to the rear of the cruiser and laid the map out flat on top of the trunk.

Miguel and the two deputies crowded around.

Abe pointed to a specific spot on the map. "We believe a friend of ours, Jack Tremens, has gone missing and is somewhere in this vicinity."

"What is that, some kind of installation?" Dobson asked.

"It's an old abandoned military site."

"What makes you think Tremens is there?" Kurtz asked.

"We've pinpointed the signal from his phone," Miguel said, holding up his own cell phone to show the officers the display on his screen. "We're using a GPS phone tracker on my phone to find him."

"How far is that?" Dobson asked.

"Another twenty or so miles," Abe said. He heard a big truck approaching from the opposite side of the road and looked up.

A semi-truck hauling a forty-foot long shipping container on a flatbed trailer barreled down the asphalt. Abe knew if he had his radar gun handy it would be an easy ticket.

"Where're they coming from?" Kurtz said. "That's the fifth one since we've been here."

The men stepped back, buffeted by the thundering big rig. No sooner had the truck gone by another one appeared, following close behind.

"What's their damn hurry," Kurtz said and turned to Abe. "Sure you don't want us to go tag their asses?"

"You can get them later." Abe figured the deputies had their dash cam on and it had recorded every license plate that had passed by. "Any questions?"

Kurtz and Dobson shook their heads. Miguel was already walking to the Bronco.

"Okay, then," Abe said. "Let's head out."

30

GRAND TOUR

Even though his gun had been confiscated, Jack felt his capturers were being a little lax not insisting his hands be bound behind his back. But then maybe Wilde and Dr. McCabe really didn't consider him much of a threat as two of their men were guarding him at gunpoint. He knew the braggarts had super egos and liked to flaunt their achievements so Jack was not surprised when they insisted on giving him the grand tour.

He had no idea what they had in store for him. As long as they wanted to prolong his detainment unharmed, he wasn't going to complain.

While at the Caudipteryx enclosure, Jack was given the opportunity to observe Dr. McCabe's technicians take down the turkey-sized dinosaurs with fast-acting tranquillizer darts. Once the bird-like creatures were sedated, a group of wranglers entered the cage, placed them on carts, and wheeled the unconscious specimens away.

Before leaving, Jack noticed the specie's nameplate on the cage with the scientific term *Caudipteryx* and the word written in Chinese just below. He didn't think much of it as they continued their excursion through Dr. McCabe's underground laboratory facility.

They went down a corridor and passed more enclosures with thick, steel bars, each reeking of excrement and the typical smells associated with creatures kept in captivity for long periods of time.

Jack spotted a nameplate with the scientific term: *Alxasaurus* on an empty enclosure. It also had the Chinese word written beneath. If he remembered right, it was a feathered dinosaur that stood about eight feet tall and was thought to be a herbivore even though it had long fingered claws which were most likely used for pulling down high branches to feed on and not for gutting prey.

He was beginning to wonder what happened to the creatures that were no longer in the cages when the group came around a bend and he heard what sounded like a harem of chimpanzees hooting and grunting.

Jack counted six ape-like creatures racing around like a gang of juvenile delinquents vying for attention inside the twenty-foot square containment. They looked like interbred baboons crossed with short-tailed macaques. Their faces were golden instead of the traditional red common with baboons. Each one had to weigh over fifty pounds. It was impossible to guess their age. Jack figured they were still youngsters by the way they played. There was no telling how big they would get.

The nameplate on the cage stated they were Xing-Xings, Chinese cryptids believed to have lived in the remote Asian jungles.

"Get this batch ready for transport," Dr. McCabe said and a man ran off down the hall.

When they came to the next cage, Dr. McCabe turned, blocking Wilde's view so he couldn't see between the bars.

"What are you doing?" Wilde said indignantly. "Out of my way."

"Okay, but you're not going to like it," Dr. McCabe said and stepped aside.

Jack glanced into the cage and saw a large creature—twelve feet from the crown of its head down to its toes—with long orangey-brown hair, sprawled on the cement. The animal was thin and bony and looked as though it had starved to death. It was lying in a pool of its own dried urine and black feces.

"Damn it, Joel," Wilde said. "They wanted this for their main attraction."

"You needn't worry," Dr. McCabe said. "I know where we can get a perfectly healthy Yeren."

"You touch Lennie and I'll—" A rifle butt to the head silenced Jack.

31

FEATHER DOWN

Maria drove the Ford F-150 up Myrtle Cooper's driveway and parked the truck a few feet away from the woman's front porch steps. She shut off the engine and turned to Nora sitting in the front passenger seat. "Maybe I should have called. I know I hate it when people just drop in."

"I'm sure it's fine," Nora said. "I hear Myrtle runs most of her business from her home anyway as she's planning to close up her shop in town."

"Really?"

"Word is her landlord is thinking of jacking up her rent."

"Money-grubber." Maria opened the driver's door and got out. She walked up the steps while Nora remained in the truck. She rapped on the front door with her bare knuckles. After waiting about ten seconds, she knocked again. Still, no one came to the door. Maria turned and looked over at Nora who had lowered the passenger window.

"Maybe she's not home," Nora called out.

"See, I knew I should have called," Maria grumbled.

"You know what? I'm sure Clare must have some goat cheese she might be willing to sell you."

"You think?" Maria replied. She came down the steps and got back into the truck.

"Besides, Abe asked if I would check in on her," Nora said.

Maria started up the engine and hung a U-turn to head back to the main road.

"Abe asked you to check up on Clare? *Clare Stone*! You've got to be kidding me. The woman's tougher than most men around here."

"I know, I know," Nora laughed. "Asking for goat cheese will be the perfect excuse to drop by."

"Aren't you the devious one."

They drove to the Stone's farm, which was a five-mile drive away.

"I was hoping Abe would have gotten back to me by now. Any word from Miguel?" Nora asked.

"No, but I wouldn't worry. They'll find Jack. I'm sure he just had engine trouble."

"Doesn't explain why he hasn't called."

"No, it doesn't."

Five minutes later, Maria turned off onto the Stone's gravel driveway. She pulled up to the side of the farmhouse and shut off the engine. This time both Maria and Nora got out of the truck. They went up and Nora knocked on the front door. She tried two more times but no one answered. "Maybe Clare and Myrtle went out somewhere together."

"Want to check around back?"

"Sure," Nora said. "Maybe Clare's tending to her goats."

They walked along the side of the farmhouse toward the pens.

"Oh my God," Maria said when she saw a dead goat compressed to the ground like it had been run over by a car. "Poor thing. What happened to it?"

"There's another one." Nora pointed to a goat lying by the fence.

Maria and Nora stepped around the corner of the house. That's when they saw a giant Thunderbird sprawled in the grass like a crashed glider.

Nora cupped her hands around her mouth and hollered, "Clare! Can you hear me?"

A dog barked from the shed.

"That's sounds like Rounder," Nora said.

They hurried over to the goat corrals and found another dead Thunderbird by the shed. Its wingspan stretched fifteen feet.

Maria spotted Rounder sitting on the ground. He was staring up at the overhang of the shed's steel roof. The tip of a giant wing hung over the edge.

Rounder turned to Maria then stared up and started to bark.

"What's he barking at?" Nora said.

Maria glanced at Nora. "You don't think..."

"I'll go find a ladder." Nora ran inside the shed and retrieved a folding ladder. She stood it up and spread apart the legs. She held it steady while Maria climbed up the rungs.

Maria got high enough so she could see onto the roof. "Oh my God."

"What is it?" Nora asked.

"It's Clare."

"Is she alive?"

"I don't know."

"I'm calling 9-1-1." Nora pulled out her cell phone and tapped in the numbers. A few seconds later the operator came on the line and asked Nora to state her emergency.

* * *

Maria and Nora stood by while three firemen removed Clare from the roof and placed her on the paramedic's collapsible gurney. She was conscious by then and explained how she had ended up on the roof. Maria remembered saying something to the effect "Clare, you're one tough broad," which sounded kind of corny when she thought about it afterward.

The paramedic that examined Clare thought she had a broken right arm and dislocated shoulder. Her ribs on the same side of her body were giving her pain. She had a massive bruise on the right side of her face. It was quite possible she had internal injuries as well as more fractures.

It was a miracle she was even alive.

They would know more after a thorough examination at the emergency room and some X-rays.

Rounder sat by Nora's feet while she and Maria watched the fire truck pull away after the ambulance.

"What now?" Maria asked.

"I can call Daren Sikes," Nora said. "He's a good friend of Abe's and sometimes offers his services to Clare's business. He could bring some men and take care of the bodies. I'm sure he'll watch over Rounder and the farm."

"Nice to have good neighbors."

"That's for sure. We better get over to the hospital and see what they find after they examine Clare. I'll call Abe when we know more."

"Boy, when it rains, it pours," Maria said. "First Jack goes missing and now Clare almost gets killed. What next?"

32

JACK'S PHONE

"Are we getting close?" Abe asked Miguel, who was staring down at the tiny screen on his cell phone.

"Unless we made a wrong turn, it seems we're driving away from Jack's position."

"Means we're on the wrong side of the base. That's okay. Instead of driving all the way around, let's enter here," Abe said, taking a right hand turn off the main highway onto a single-lane road that journeyed into the forest. "We can cut through to the other side. It'll be quicker."

The cracked and weathered asphalt appeared to have been paved more than half a century ago though Miguel spotted fresh patches of dark tar along the way, covering potholes recently filled in. Someone had been maintaining this road. He glanced at his side mirror and saw the deputies trailing behind.

Bright sunlight glared on the windshield as they suddenly came out of the trees and entered a clearing.

"Oh, I don't believe it," Abe said, veering to the right and slamming on the brakes so as not to hit a twelve-foot high chain-link fence with coiled razor wire blocking their path.

Abe and Miguel climbed out of the Bronco.

The deputy cruiser pulled up alongside. Dobson and Kurtz got out.

"This is it?" Dobson said as if disappointed.

They stared through the steel mesh at the abandoned Army base. It was a wonder the buildings were still standing. Every window of the two-story barracks was shattered and sections of the roof were either bowed or caved in. Three other structures with weathered exteriors were in worse condition and looked as though they might topple easily under a stiff wind.

Mother Nature had been persistent in reclaiming what was rightfully hers.

Tall weeds sprouted from every fissure in the cement; creeper vines embedded in the walls like a bad case of acne.

The parking lot transformed into a field, the rusted shell of a troop carrier partially hidden in the overgrown grass.

Miguel spotted a concrete structure beyond the rundown buildings. "What do you make of that?" he asked and pointed through the fence.

"Might possibly be the entrance to the underground bunker," Abe said.

"So what's the plan?" Kurtz asked.

Miguel could tell the young deputy was getting antsy. He also noticed there was a large chain securing the main gate. "Hope someone brought bolt cutters."

"Never leave home without them," Kurtz said. He walked to the rear of the cruiser, opened the trunk, and took out a pair of heavy-duty cutters. He came over and inspected the chain securing the gate. "This is weird. This chain looks fairly new."

"You're right," Miguel said, noticing the contrast between the rusted fence and the chain that looked like it had recently been purchased. "Just like someone's been repairing that road."

"Which confirms that McCabe might be operating from here," Abe said.

It took Kurtz a few seconds to snip through the chain.

"Okay, everyone. Gear up," Abe said.

Miguel followed the sheriff to the rear of the Bronco. Abe opened the back and handed Miguel a Stevens Model 69RXL pump shotgun with a box of .12 gauge shells.

The sheriff took the Remington shotgun for himself and stuffed his vest pockets with cartridges.

Both men checked their side arms and made sure they were loaded.

Besides their Glocks, the deputies had armed themselves with Ithaca MAG-10 Roadblocker combat shotguns. Each man wore a bulletproof vest. Kurtz went a step further and was wearing a tactical helmet with chinstraps.

"You boys certainly came prepared," Abe said.

"Never underestimate the enemy," Kurtz said.

Dobson smiled at the sheriff. "Frank thinks it's better to come loaded for bear than to end up its lunch."

"Obviously. There's no telling what we'll find, so I suggest everyone stay alert," Abe said.

"You mean stay frosty," Kurtz said, ratcheting a round in the chamber.

"Sure thing, snowman," Dobson said deadpan as though they were a comedy team and he was the straight man for Kurtz's one-liners.

Entering the compound, Miguel followed right behind the sheriff while the two deputies spread out and guarded the flanks.

A covey of spooked grouse burst into the air from behind a bush a few feet from Kurtz. He spun around and put the fleeing flock in his sights like a trap shooter targeting a quick volley of clay birds, but didn't fire.

"Thaw, Frosty," Dobson quipped.

"You're just jealous you don't have my razor-sharp reflexes."

"I think that chinstrap's cutting off the blood supply to your brain."

"Cut the chatter," Abe said, breaking up their routine.

Miguel glanced at his phone then looked to the area to his right. "The signal seems to be coming from that direction."

"Do you want to check it out?" Abe asked.

"What about the bunker?"

"We'll split up. Take Dobson with you," the sheriff said. "Kurtz and I will see if we can find a way into the bunker."

"All right," Miguel said. Dobson joined him and they walked toward the fence line perimeter. Searching for a way into the forest, Miguel was thankful when they found a section crushed under a fallen tree and they didn't have to try scaling the fence and deal with the injurious razor wire.

"So this Tremens, is he a good friend of yours?" Dobson asked as they walked along the horizontal tree trunk.

"You could say that. We've known each other for years. We even spent some time together as cryptid hunters," Miguel replied, jumping down onto solid ground.

"No kidding."

"If we knew then what we know now neither of us would have ever taken those jobs."

After hiking a hundred yards, Miguel stopped and gazed at the tracking app on his screen. "This is the spot. Jack's phone must be around here somewhere."

Dobson looked down and began kicking away at the debris on the ground.

Miguel stepped over to the base of a tree. He knelt down and felt around a small pile of dried pine needles. His fingers touched a familiar shape. "I found it!"

"Good eye," Dobson said.

Miguel heard the muffled sound of a racing engine. He glanced around but there was no vehicle in sight. "Do you hear that?"

"Yeah," Dobson replied. "Where the hell is it coming from?"

Before Miguel could answer, an SUV appeared out of nowhere like it had been catapulted out of the ground and slammed into the deputy, tossing him into the air.

Dobson came down on the roof of the vehicle, bounced off, and landed hard on the ground.

The SUV skidded to a stop. The front passenger door swung open and a big man in a business suit got out. He walked back, stood over Dobson, and aimed a Uzi pistol at the deputy's head.

Miguel stepped out from behind a tree, yelled, "Hey, shit for brains!" and fired his shotgun, blowing the big man off his feet.

The driver in the SUV gunned the engine and sped off through the trees.

Pumping another cartridge into the chamber, Miguel rushed over to Dobson. He knelt and could tell the young man was dead by the vacant stare in his eyes.

"Shit." Miguel drew his hand down over Dobson's face, closing his eyelids.

Miguel went over to the man sprawled on the ground. He had a basketball-sized hole in his chest and his shredded white shirt was steadily turning red from the blood gurgling out of the massive wound. The man wore a button on his lapel with the letters WE: Wilde Enterprises.

Miguel walked over to where the SUV first appeared and saw the ramp stretching down into an underground tunnel.

He'd found the entrance to the bunker.

33

DOBHAR-CHU

"These look like those trucks we saw earlier," Deputy Kurtz said once they had reached the backside of the barracks and saw three semi-trucks with flatbed trailers parked next to half a dozen shipping containers.

"Let's take a closer look," Abe said. He wasn't so much interested in the trucks as he was in the sea vans. He stepped over to a 20-foot long freight container next to the longer 40-footers. The twin doors were partially open so he peeked inside. "Kurtz, come see this."

Kurtz poked his head in. "Looks like a setup for human trafficking."

The interior of the container was subdivided into two sections by steel bars with a cage door. The area in the rear looked like a zoo habitat as there were feeding troughs and the floor was covered with straw.

The forward half was designed for a person, as it had a bunk, portable toilet, washbasin, and a small refrigerator. An air-conditioning unit was mounted on the ceiling.

"Not people," Abe said. "Animals. The accommodations are for whoever's job it is to look after them while they're being transported."

Abe and Kurtz checked two other cargo containers and found them to have similar layouts inside.

"Notice anything strange on the doors?" Abe said.

"Yeah, everything is labeled in Chinese."

"Could be the intended destination. Let's keep going."

As they got closer to what they believed to be the entrance to the bunker, Abe saw another fence blocking their path, only this one had signs posted—WARNING—ELECTRIC FENCE.

"Now what?" Kurtz said.

"Hold this." Abe handed his shotgun to the deputy. He unbuckled his leather belt and pulled it out of the loops. He showed Kurtz the metal buckle with the American eagle. "Stand back."

Kurtz stood behind Abe.

Abe held the belt by the leather end and swung the buckle at the fence.

Nothing happened; the power was turned off.

"Up and over," Abe said, putting his belt back on. He held the shotguns and watched Kurtz scale the fence and drop to the other side. Abe ejected the shells from the shotguns so when he threw each one over, there was not a chance of either firing accidentally.

Abe clawed his way up the fence, slipped over the top, and dropped to the ground.

While they reloaded their guns, Abe noticed Kurtz staring strangely at the bunker. "What is it?"

"There's a damn moat."

A ten-foot wide strip of murky water prevented them from reaching the entrance.

Kurtz grinned at Abe. "What do you think is in there: man-eating sharks or piranhas? Hope you brought your swim trunks."

Abe looked a little further down and spotted a long wooden plank spanning the broad ditch. "I don't think we need to worry about getting wet. We can cross there."

When they got to the edge of the makeshift bridge, Abe noticed the water level was almost to the lip of the moat and only a few inches from touching the bottom of the crude pedestrian crossing.

Kurtz went first and was almost halfway across when Abe noticed the water rippling by the deputy's feet.

Abe shouted, "Kurtz, look out!" but by then it was too late.

A giant otter lurched out of the murky moat and landed on the thick plank directly in front of Kurtz.

Instead of smooth skin, the enormous gator-sized creature had overlapping scales covering most of its body. The head was extremely large, and when it opened its mouth, it growled like a dog, revealing a set of vicious canine teeth.

The front legs were slightly shorter than its hind legs and it had a long tapered tail that was as long as its body.

Abe could hear the plank begin to crack with the added weight.

Kurtz raised his shotgun to fire upon the creature. The otter was lightning fast and dove at Kurtz, knocking him off the plank and taking him under the water.

Aiming his shotgun where Kurtz had gone in, Abe hoped the creature would come up for air so he could get a shot but the water soon became calm.

"Damn it." Abe laid down his shotgun and drew his revolver. He was about to jump in when he heard a loud splash behind him. He half turned realizing the cunning predator must have swum under the plank to attack him from behind.

The giant otter propelled out of the water.

Abe stumbled back unable to keep his balance and fell on the edge of the concrete.

And then came a loud blast.

The top of the otter's head blew apart showering Abe with bloody bits. The creature's upper body fell across the plank leaving its back legs to dangle in the water.

Miguel stood ten feet away and pumped another round in his shotgun. "You okay?"

"Yeah, but it got Kurtz." Abe looked down at the water and saw the deputy drift to the surface in an oily ring of blood. He was facedown, his arms floating out from his side.

The otter had ripped a large chunk out of his neck. Abe watched the severed carotid artery pump out the man's lifeblood for the last beat.

Abe glared at the dead creature and gave it a kick. "What the hell is that?"

"It's called a Dobhar-chu," Miguel said. "It's Irish for *water hound.*"

"Is this another one of McCabe's abominations?"

"That would be my guess."

"Where's Dobson?" Abe asked.

"Dead."

"Jesus, how?"

"He was run over. There's a tunnel on the other side of the base. I think it leads to an underground garage maybe to the bunker."

"Did you see who did it?"

"The windows were tinted. I did manage to kill one when he got out to finish the job. He was working for Wilde Enterprises. I feel really bad about Dobson and Kurtz."

"So do I. I liked those boys." Abe holstered his revolver and picked up his shotgun. "Let's hope they didn't die for nothing."

34

THE PLATFORM

Agent Hunter waited until Nick and Meg were safely in the elevator before pushing the button for the hotel lobby. "There's a car waiting downstairs. We should be there in thirty minutes assuming we don't hit too much traffic."

Meg turned to Nick and straightened out his tie. "Can't let you go in there looking like a scruff. I really wish you would have brought another tie." Against her objections, Nick had insisted on packing the red tie with the black polka dots, which screamed to be noticed with his gray sharkskin suit.

"I doubt anyone is going to notice my tie when I'm sitting behind a microphone," Nick said.

Agent Hunter put his hand up to his earpiece. "All right. Then we'll take the Metro."

"Is something wrong?" Meg asked.

"Change of plans," Hunter said. "Protesters have blocked our intended route."

"What are they protesting?" Nick asked.

"Climate change, immigration, health care. Who knows?"

A chime sounded and the car came to a stop. The elevator doors slid open.

Special Agent Rivers stood outside the elevator. "Follow me. We're going out the back way through the service entrance."

Hunter escorted Nick and Meg out. They stayed behind Rivers as she turned down a side corridor.

Pushing through a door, they hustled into the hotel's laundry where employees were unloading white canvas carts and shoving dirty linen into industrial-sized washing machines.

Meg could feel the humidity on her face from the steam presses.

Rivers grabbed the bar on the Exit Only door. She went out first, followed by Meg and Nick. Hunter stepped outside and they scurried down the alleyway.

"Stay close," Rivers said. "The Metro station is less than a block away."

They entered the throng of pedestrians on the sidewalk and kept to a brisk pace but not too hurried to draw unwanted attention.

The sidewalk entrance led them down a flight of stairs to the turnstiles for the underground rail. Rivers swiped a special SmarTrip fare card on the access reader and waved everyone through. They continued to an escalator that took them down to the passenger platform where over a hundred people were standing waiting for the next train.

Meg gazed up and marveled at the arched "waffle" style architecture in the tunnel, reminding her of being inside a futuristic city. "This place is amazing."

"I'll say," Nick said, craning his neck at the ceiling.

"Welcome to the Washington Metropolitan Area Transit Authority," Hunter said, sounding like a proud tour guide. "Its one of the busiest rapid transit systems in the country. Average ridership is about 600,000 a day."

"That is impressive," Meg said. She was beginning to feel a little claustrophobic being stuck between all these people.

"Mack, we have company," Rivers said.

Meg saw the agents staring at a small group of six coming down the escalator. They were dressed in black with hoods and wore partial animal masks covering their noses and chins.

"Oh shit," Mack said.

"What's wrong?" Nick asked.

"We've got trouble." Mack reached inside his jacket and stepped in front of Meg and Nick.

Meg looked over the agent's shoulder and saw the hooded men steadily approaching in their direction.

The hooded figures stormed through the crowd like a black wedge. Meg saw the one leading the pack slip his hand into his sweatshirt pocket and pull out a gun.

"GET DOWN!" Rivers yelled. Everyone around them immediately dropped to the floor. Mack had his gun out and was pointing it at the men marching through the cowering people hoping to stay out of the line of fire.

A train emerged out of the tunnel and came to a sudden stop alongside the platform. The side doors automatically opened. Before the passengers could step out, a swarm of frightened people scrambled to their feet and rushed the train.

The Cryptos drew their weapons and opened up on the agents.

A barrage of bullets zinged over everyone's heads, striking the side of the train, and punching pockmarks into the surrounding ceramic pilings.

A Crypto wearing a balaclava Bigfoot facemask grabbed a young girl by the back of her jacket and used her for a shield as he fired his handgun.

Mack didn't hesitate and shot the creep in the kneecap. The man let go of the girl and stumbled forward. Mack finished him off with a bullet to the head.

Two Cryptos dashed behind a thick stanchion for cover. They leaned out from opposite sides and fired.

Rivers picked off an assailant as the other ducked out of sight. She clutched her Glock in a two-handed grip and marched toward the upright. A man in a Thunderbird mask poked his head out to take another shot and Rivers nailed him twice in the chest.

"Get on the train," Hunter yelled to Meg and Nick.

Nick pulled Meg but there were too many frantic people trying to squeeze into the train. "It's no use," Nick yelled to the agent.

Hunter turned and shouted to Rivers who was about to line up a shot on a Crypto backing towards the escalator. "Anna, help them out!"

Rivers glanced over at Hunter and nodded she understood. She ran up the middle like a linebacker and opened up a path through the manic crowd so Nick and Meg could worm their way onto the train. The agent managed to fit in as the doors began to close.

Meg glanced out the window as they pulled away and saw Hunter running after the radicals racing up the escalator. She couldn't stop shaking.

Nick wrapped his arms around her and said. "What the hell did I get us into?"

35

MUTANT WARFARE

"You were right, this does look like a way in," Miguel said after he helped Abe muscle open the heavy bunker door and saw the steps leading down into the pitch dark.

After pulling Kurtz from the water and covering him with an old tarp they found discarded by some oil drums, Miguel and Abe planned to collect Dobson's body later once they had rescued Jack.

That is if Jack was even here and everything went off without a hitch. Somehow Miguel doubted it would be that easy.

Miguel followed Abe down the gloomy stairwell into an underground passageway arched with masonry brick and sparsely lit dome lights staggered along the ceiling.

He saw 24-inch-sized stenciled letters on the walls that signified something but Miguel hadn't a clue what they meant. They reached a junction that split off into three different directions. Each way led down a cavernous thoroughfare into more darkness.

Miguel remembered a Halloween night when he and Maria had taken their daughter to a festival held on a farm. Sophia had run into a cornfield, got turned around, and couldn't find her way out. It had taken Miguel and Maria twenty agonizing minutes searching with flashlights, calling out her name and worrying before they finally found her sitting on the ground, crying, which made Miguel wonder if the sheriff and he would share the same fate and end up getting lost in this network of subterranean tunnels.

"It's like a damn maze down here," Abe said, his voice cutting into Miguel's thoughts.

Miguel was about to comment when they stepped into a large chamber with a twenty-foot high vaulted ceiling that forked down two other corridors and were wide enough to drive a semi-truck and trailer through. "This must be where they load up the vehicles."

Someone yelled from further away, followed by a gunshot.

"This way," Abe said. He held his shotgun across his chest and dashed down the tunnel. It was wide enough that Miguel didn't have to follow behind and could run beside the sheriff.

Miguel spotted a bank of windows to his right. He glanced inside and saw a dimly lit laboratory with scientific equipment and examination tables. The blue glow of an X-ray reader was on the wall displaying a skeletal cranium Miguel believed to be simian.

Another shot rang out, this time much closer.

They came to a bend and turned the corner.

A man in an orange jumpsuit was aiming a rifle barrel between the bars of a cage.

"Drop the gun!" Abe shouted.

The man turned with a surprised look on his face.

"I won't tell you again."

A large, black-leathery hand reached out, grabbed the man by the nape of the neck, and yanked the man's head between the steel bars, crushing his skull.

Miguel heard a bone-twisting crack like a turkey leg being wrenched from the carcass. The rifle fell to the concrete floor, followed by the headless man.

A cage door burst open and slammed back against the steel bars.

Miguel watched a hunched ape-like creature stagger out.

"What the hell is that?" Abe asked.

It looked to be around six hundred pounds.

Miguel's first thought was that it was a silverback gorilla.

When it limped into the dim light, he could see its body was covered with long, dirty white hair. It seemed to be in extreme pain, possibly suffering from a deformity to its spine. "I think it's some kind of mutant. Must be why the guy was trying to kill it."

The creature gazed at Miguel and the sheriff with a pathetic look in its eyes. It snarled and came at them on all fours in a determined knuckle walk.

Miguel hesitated, feeling sorry for the creature as Abe fired his shotgun. The heavy gauge pellets pulverized the creature's face and neck. It took two faltering steps and crashed onto the cement floor. A pool of blood formed around the shredded head.

"Jesus," Abe said, gazing down at the dead animal. "Is this what he's been creating?"

Miguel shook his head. "Not intentionally. This must be one of McCabe's rejects."

Another giant ape came out of the cage.

It weighed about the same as the one Abe had killed, only this animal was standing erect and stood eight feet tall. It too, had long white hair. The black orb eyes were weepy and its chin was slobbered with yellowish drool.

"What are these things? This one looks sick," Abe said, sliding the pump action back on his shotgun.

"I'm pretty sure they're Yetis," Miguel said.

The Yeti glared at Miguel and Abe then let out a deep-throated roar.

Three more Siberian Snowmen lumbered out into the passageway, each one stricken with some type of disfigurement.

Miguel could hear more of them moving about inside the caged area like huddled lepers hiding in a cave.

"I don't think we have enough fire power to take them all down," Abe said.

"Then we better run!" Miguel yelled. He turned and bolted down the corridor with the sheriff running by his side.

He could hear the rest of the Yetis in the caged area, funneling out into the passageway and stomping after them.

Miguel and Abe darted around the corner and came to a sudden halt when they met up with a dozen men in orange jumpsuits. Some men carried hunting rifles while the other men were busily attaching incendiary bomb devices to the walls.

The armed men immediately turned their guns on Miguel and Abe just as the troop of Yetis stormed around the corner.

Miguel and Abe dove behind a cargo box a few feet from the wall to avoid being cut down by the hail of bullets.

The Yetis's yowls could be heard over the steady barrage of gunfire.

And then a man screamed.

Miguel peeked over the top of the crate.

A Yeti picked the screaming man up off of his feet, sinking its teeth into the top of his head like it was biting into a chocolate Easter bunny.

Two Yetis attacked a man, ripping him apart as though he were a scarecrow made of straw limbs.

A bloody Yeti riddled with bullets managed to fall onto the gunman shooting it.

The concrete floor was becoming increasingly slick with blood from the fallen bodies.

More men screamed as the beasts overpowered them.

"Let's get out of here," Abe said, nudging Miguel's arm. They got up from their hiding place and darted down another tunnel away from the fracas.

Entering a narrow corridor, Miguel heard someone call out his name.

"What took you guys so long?" Jack asked. He was standing inside an enclosure with both hands wrapped around the steel bars.

Miguel used the butt of his shotgun and struck the padlock securing the cage door. The lock broke away and Miguel swung open the door so Jack could step out.

"You know, it might have been simpler if you had used your phone to call us," Miguel said.

"I was afraid if they found it on me they would take it away." "Makes sense. Here, take my gun," Miguel said and handed Jack the Desert Eagle from his holster. "We have to hurry. I think they're planning to blow this place."

As if on cue, Miguel heard a loud explosion and the ceiling rained dust as the ground under his boots shook.

"Is there another way out?" Abe asked.

"Yes," Jack said. "We can go out by the parking garage."

Miguel and Abe followed Jack down the corridor.

"We have to warn Nora," Jack shouted over his shoulder.

"Why's that?" Miguel answered, running behind him.

"I think McCabe is sending men to kidnap Lennie."

"What the hell for?" Abe yelled to be heard over the rumbling.

"I'm not sure but it has something to do with Carter Wilde."

Miguel heard another explosion and felt a wave of heat on his back.

More bombs went off systematically throughout the tunnels as the underground military base erupted into a fiery inferno.

36

OFF- ROADER

"Are you sure this is the right way?" Alice asked from the front seat as they entered a complex of three-story business buildings with large parking lots on the frontages.

Toby gazed into the rearview mirror at Laney sitting in the backseat with Allen.

Laney held up the envelope containing the supposed rejection notice from the FDA. "2752 Hi-Tech Way. Suite 201."

"Well, this is Hi-Tech Way," Toby confirmed. He opened his hands and flexed his fingers before gripping the steering wheel.

When they reached the designated address, Toby turned into the near-vacant parking lot and shut off the Barracuda. "This can't be right?"

Laney and Allen leaned forward and looked through the windshield at the granite sign posted on a grassy knoll—NEW AGE LABORATORIES: A DIVISON OF WILDE ENTERPRISES. 2752 HI-TECH WAY.

"I thought you said this would be the FDA's Center for Drug and Research?" Toby asked.

"That's what we were led to believe."

"Why would the envelope have this as a return address?" Laney asked.

"Someone must have goofed up when they sent it out and forgot to put on a bogus one," Allen replied. "Stupid on their part but fortunate for us. Maybe we can finally get to the bottom of what is going on."

"What, you really think someone is actually working in there?" Toby said.

Laney had to agree with Toby. Even though the building appeared fully constructed, there were still workmen walking in and out of the front lobby. A small crew of landscapers was planting shrubs along the base of the building.

Several trucks with ramps on their tailgates were parked in a turnaround close to the lobby entrance. Laney watched moving men shoving office furniture on carts.

"Someone's texting me," Alice said and looked at her cell phone.

"Who is it?" Toby asked.

"It's the senior center. Oh my God."

"What's wrong?" Laney asked.

"It's Harvey," Alice said. "He's back in the hospital."

"He looked perfectly fine when we had lunch with him," Toby said.

"His wife says the cancer is back and to please send our prayers."

"I don't understand. I thought he was cured." Toby turned in his seat to face Allen. "He's cured. I mean we all are, right?"

Laney saw a stoic look on Allen's face even though an emerald tear streamed down his green cheek. "Allen, are you okay?"

"I'm so sorry Toby and Alice," Allen said. "I really believed it would work for the long term."

"And here I thought my fingers were aching from the long drive," Toby said, glancing over at Alice.

"I didn't want to say anything. I thought it was just carsickness."

"So, all this time we were just guinea pigs," Toby said, unable to contain his anger.

"Toby! Allen would never do that!" Laney said. "He loves you guys."

"I'm sorry, Allen," Toby apologized. "That was wrong of me."

"I don't blame you for being angry," Allen said. "I really thought I had found the cure."

"Cure or not, Allen, your plants give us hope," Alice said.

"I think you and the others deserve more than just a little hope. Alice, if you would, Laney and I need to get out."

"Sure, Allen." Alice opened her door and climbed out while Allen pushed the front seat forward and got out of the car.

Laney scooted across the backseat and got out as well.

Allen put the seat back so Alice could get into the car. He leaned down on the window frame so he could see Toby sitting behind the wheel. "Keep an eye out for trouble."

"So what's the plan?" Toby asked.

"Laney and I are going to sneak in and see what we can find in Suite 201."

* * *

112

As they were dressed in sweatshirts and jeans, Laney and Allen easily posed as the movers, and when there was no one around, they scurried up the ramp of a truck and wheeled out a large desk on casters.

Laney was shocked to see a security guard sitting behind a big counter in the center of the lobby when they entered the building. Allen pushed from behind keeping his head down so his face couldn't be seen while Laney guided the front of the desk and steered for the elevators to the right of the granite stairs that led up to the second floor with a wraparound glass banister.

"Hey, you two. Where do you think *you're* going?"

Laney froze in a panic. She turned slowly and saw the security guard stand up.

"Well?" the man persisted.

"We...we were," Laney stammered, knowing their cover was blown.

"Use the freight elevator," the security guard said and jabbed his thumb over his shoulder at the opposite side of the lobby.

"Oh, yeah, sorry," Laney replied. She pulled the front of the desk around in a slow turn as Allen pushed.

Laney gave the security guard a sheepish grin as they passed the counter to the open doors of the freight elevator. She stepped aside and let Allen shove the desk inside the spacious car.

She pushed the button for the second floor. She noticed buttons P1 and P2 below the button marked L for lobby. "Strange to have two underground garage levels *and* a parking lot out front."

"Must have a lot of employees," Allen said. "This is weird."

"What is?"

"I'm feeling a tingle." Allen shivered for a moment. "It's gone now."

A chime sounded and the elevator doors opened to the sound of someone drilling.

They pushed the desk out into a long carpeted hallway with office doors on either side and parked the piece of furniture against the wall. A few workers were running wiring and putting up ceiling panels.

Laney and Allen headed down the corridor in the opposite direction, noting the suite numbers on the doors.

"It's down this way," Laney said.

They soon reached Suite 201. Laney tried the lever handle. The door was locked. She stepped aside and watched Allen insert his finger into the locking mechanism. He popped the tumblers and the door clicked open.

Inside was a large room of ten partitioned cubicles and a single office with a glass door and windows covered by white blinds.

"Best bet will be the office," Allen said.

Again, the door was locked. Allen picked the lock in two seconds.

Laney went over to the desk to search the in- and out-baskets while Allen rummaged through the bookshelves next to a wall of filing cabinets.

Allen pulled out a bound document and began leafing through the pages. "This is the company's business plan."

"What does it say?" Laney asked, not bothering to look up as she examined the paperwork in the bins.

"This facility has been set up for conducting clinical trials and research to assist the Federal Drug Administration in an outsourcing capacity."

"Isn't that a conflict of interest being that this company is a subsidiary run by Wilde Enterprises which is also a leading pharmaceutical company?"

"It would certainly seem that way," Allen replied, putting the binder back on the shelf. He went over to the filing cabinet and pulled open a drawer labeled M-O. He pulled out a folder with the last name Moss. "Bingo!"

"What did you find?" Laney asked.

"It's a file with our name on it." He opened the folder. "It's got our application and everything. There's even a copy of the phony rejection letter they sent us." Allen reached in and pulled out another folder, and looked inside. "Here's another one for someone else. Oh my God, Laney. Somehow Wilde Enterprises is intercepting people's applications for FDA approvals and stealing their research."

"We have to find a way to stop them."

"And we will," Allen said, gathering up more files for evidence.

"I think I found something." Laney showed Allen a shipping invoice. "The shipping address; isn't this the same place that incinerated our plants?"

"Let me see." Allen looked at the invoice. "You're right."

"The signature at the bottom was dated yesterday. Allen, I just had a thought."

"What's that?"

"I think we need to go down to the parking garages."

They wasted no time and rushed out, making sure they left everything the same way they found it—minus a few incriminating files.

Upon reaching the freight elevator, they discovered the doors closed as someone was coming up. They hurried across the broad landing overlooking the downstairs lobby and grabbed a passenger elevator down to the first parking garage level.

When they stepped out, they saw a small fleet of white vans all facing the wall, parked together side by side.

"I'm getting that tingling sensation again," Allen said. He jogged over to the vehicles and stopped behind the fourth van. He worked his magic tripping the lock and swung open the back doors.

Laney took a look inside and gasped, "Oh my God, Allen."

"Oh my God is right," Allen beamed.

"So it was all a trick to make you think it was all destroyed so they could patent it for themselves."

"Looks that way."

The van was filled completely with bundles of Allen's cure-all plants.

37

WORMHOLE

"Is anyone hurt?" Anna yelled, trying desperately to be heard over the clamoring passengers crammed in the subway car. The people closest to her glanced her way and shook their heads with wide-eyed expressions on their faces. Everyone was holding onto poles and seatback railings as the subway train thundered through the dark tunnel like a high-speed bullet traveling down a gun barrel.

"I think we're coming to a stop," Nick said, his cheek pressed against the window glass so he could see where they were going.

Those that heard him immediately shoved their way toward the side doors.

Instead of stopping, the train raced on through, ignoring the crowd standing on the platform.

"Hey, that's the second station we've passed," a man yelled out.

Meg grabbed Anna by the sleeve. "Why didn't we stop?"

"I don't know. I'm going forward to speak to the engineer," Anna said, not wanting to start a panic and tell her there was a good chance they were on a runaway train. "I'll be right back."

Anna weaved her way through the passengers blocking the aisle and reached the narrow door. She banged on the door with the heel of her fist. "Hello in there. Open up. This is the FBI." When no one answered, she took a step back and kicked just to the left of the door handle.

The door banged open.

Anna was immediately buffeted by a strong wind blowing through the gaping hole in the shattered windshield. The engineer was slumped forward on the blood drenched control panel.

She took a step inside the driver's cab and stumbled. She looked down and saw baseball-sized chunks of concrete strewn on the deck.

Something struck a portion of the still-intact windshield causing Anna to flinch.

She stared through the glass and saw large pieces of cement raining down from the tunnel's ceiling in the beam of the train's headlights.

Anna pulled the dead engineer from his chair onto the floor.

She sat in his seat and studied the control panel. The engineer had pushed the thrust lever all the way forward after being struck in the head by the hail of concrete smashing through the windshield.

Anna placed her left hand on the edge of the control panel to brace herself and grabbed the T-shaped lever with her right. She knew if she pulled back abruptly there was a good chance the train would come to a screeching halt and derail.

She steadily pulled back and looked out the windshield.

The train was approaching a bend. At the speed the train was currently going, it would jump off the rails and slam into the tunnel wall.

She had no choice but to yank back on the thruster lever.

The steel wheels on the tracks locked up with a loud squeal of screeching metal.

Anna saw a huge section of the tunnel wall punch out as a massive creature slithered out and blocked the train tracks.

The humongous Mongolian death worm turned its eyeless head, drawn to the vibration of the oncoming train, and opened its circular mouth rimmed with spear-length teeth like it could swallow it whole. The vile monster's girth was almost as large as the circumference of the tunnel. A thick salivary goop spewed from its mouth and flew at the windshield. Anna knew the venom would be deadly if it got on her skin.

She jumped off the seat and darted through the open doorway into the passenger car, screaming as she dove for the floor, "Everyone get down. We're about to crash!"

The explosive impact buckled the passenger car like a beer can being crushed while screaming passengers flew over the seats and the lights went out, pitching the interior into total darkness.

* * *

Nick woke up to a bright light shining in his face. When he raised his hand to shield his eyes, his fingers brushed the side of his face and came away sticky from the blood trickling down from a scrape on his forehead.

"Mr. Wells, can you hear me?"

"What?" Nick couldn't quite place the voice.

"Nick, are you okay?"

This time he recognized Meg as the one speaking.

"Yeah, I think so," he responded groggily.

"We have to get out of here!"

He felt two hands grab each of his wrists and haul him to his feet.

Meg and Agent Rivers stood in front of him, looking him up and down as if expecting to see shrapnel or bones sticking out of his body.

He could smell smoke and his eyes burned from the harsh odor of burning rubber and scorched metal. He glanced to his right and saw the adjoining passenger car engulfed in flames, which at the moment was the flickering light illuminating the inside of the cabin.

A few passengers were struggling to get up; some of them using the flashlight apps on their cell phones to see. Many of them were either unconscious or dead, lying heaped on the deck.

Nick heard the injured that were awake, moaning and screaming.

"Nick, we need a hand!" Agent Rivers and Meg were attempting to use a grab rail pole to jimmy the subway car door. They had managed to wedge the tip between the edge of the sliding door and the doorjamb but were unable to force the door open.

Nick joined in and the three of them were able to force the door wide enough to climb through. He looked over his shoulder and shouted, "Here's a way out!"

Agent Rivers jumped down on the ground and helped Meg out. Nick followed right behind. Half a dozen other people clambered out.

"You won't get any reception down here but you can use your phones as flashlights," Agent Rivers said to the group. "Whatever you do, stay clear of the third rail. It's the hot rail."

"What if we touch it?" a woman asked.

"You'll get electrocuted."

"What's that god-awful smell?" asked a man, the front of his shirt covered in so much blood that it couldn't possibly be his.

Nick smelled it too. It was enough to make him want to throw up.

Agent Rivers panned her flashlight around the inside of the tunnel. A mucus-like gore was dripping down the walls and was the source of the smell. "It's what's left of the Mongolian death worm we hit."

"Man, that's gross," a teenage boy said.

"How do we get out of here?" Nick asked the FBI agent.

"There should be an access ladder somewhere up ahead that we can use to get to the street."

Nick heard a few people coughing. The smoke from the burning car was drifting in their direction.

"What about the people trapped inside?" Meg asked.

"A rescue team is on the way. As soon as the train derailed, an alert was activated in the Metro control room to send help. Right now, we need to get out of here." Agent Rivers signaled for everyone to follow her.

They hadn't gone more than fifty feet when a woman screamed from the rear of the line.

Nick turned around and saw the woman on the ground, kicking her feet as an eight-foot long tubular creature began to swallow her whole, beginning with her head and shoulders.

"Jesus, what is that thing?" a man yelled.

Nick saw the ground undulating under the glow of the distant fire.

Agent Rivers shined her flashlight back in the direction of the burning subway car.

The passageway was crawling with similar creatures.

"Jesus," Agent Rivers said. "We must be near a nesting bed. Those are infant death worms."

"We have to help her," Meg said, staring at the gluttonous worm engorging the woman.

"There's nothing we can do," Agent Rivers said. "She's already dead from the worm's venom."

Nick turned and noticed the ground rippling further down the tunnel. "Uh, I think we have a problem."

Agent Rivers spun around and shined her flashlight. The edge of the beam fell on the monstrous black heads of more newly born death worms repeatedly contracting and relaxing the muscles in their skin to propel themselves forward.

A huge worm touched the third rail and immediately ignited in a shower of bright sparks with a loud *crackling* sound, the electrocuted creature liquefying right before their eyes.

"There's a way up," Agent Rivers shouted.

Nick saw her pointing to a door in the tunnel wall on the concrete berm four feet above ground.

Everyone ran toward the door, jumping over the train tracks. The teenage boy tripped and fell across the hot rail, jerking spasmodically as 600 volts electrified his body.

Agent Rivers pulled herself up onto the berm and opened the access door. She turned to Nick as he pushed Meg up and then climbed up himself. Four other people scrambled up the concrete.

"Follow me," the FBI agent said, starting up the rungs.

Nick looked back and saw the worms creeping up the concrete and edging over the lip.

The last man in line screamed.

His right leg was inside a death worm's savage mouth.

Everyone scrambled to get on the ladder. The creatures squeezed through the doorway and began to pile one on top of the other in order to reach the nearest person on the lowest rung.

"Please, hurry!" begged the woman down below.

Nick looked up past Meg and saw Agent Rivers near the top of the ladder.

A steel grill was blocking her way. Nick could see sunlight filtering down and hear protesters chanting on the street above.

Agent Rivers pushed up on the grill but it wouldn't budge. She looked down and shouted to everyone stuck on the ladder, "The grate's stuck. We're trapped!"

38

LAYING A TRAP

Nora stood at the kitchen sink, washing dishes when she heard the first vehicle pull up on the property. She glanced out the window and saw a large moving van drive toward the edge of the trees and stop.

Two black SUVs came up the driveway and pulled up next to the van. The doors opened and a dozen men got out. Some of them were armed with assault weapons. Two men were carrying lighter-weight rifles—tranquilizer guns.

Nora saw the familiar Wilde Enterprises logo on the side of the van.

They could only be here for one thing.

Lennie.

The back roll-up door on the moving van was raised. Nets and long poles with lassoes on the ends were dragged out of the cargo hold.

Nora watched three men split up from the mustering group and head toward the house. She had no idea if they intended to harm her or just wanted her cooperation in capturing Lennie. Either way, she'd be damned if she was going to give them the satisfaction.

She moved back from the window so not to be seen by the men outside. She went across the kitchen, opened the pantry door, and stepped inside, closing the door behind her. She reached up and pulled down the chain to turn on the overhead light bulb.

A loud crash of breaking glass came from the other side of the house as the men kicked in the front door.

Nora bent down and grabbed a recessed ring in the hardwood floor. Being as quiet as possible, she raised the trapdoor.

Heavy footsteps stormed through the house. Something was knocked over and toppled to the floor.

Climbing down the ladder leading to the root cellar, Nora lowered the access hatch over her head. She stepped off the last rung onto the dirt ground.

Nora knew she had only precious seconds before the men discovered the trapdoor in the pantry.

She debated grabbing the carbine leaning against the wall next to the shelves with jars of preservatives and canned goods. She knew she would be no match against the heavily armed men topside and didn't want to escalate the situation so she left the rifle behind.

She stooped and followed the narrow tunnel that stretched under the back of the property that Jack had excavated by a contractor friend and his crew for such an emergency.

Twenty seconds later, she reached the ladder at the end of the passageway.

She climbed up to the top, listened for a moment, and then pushed away a camouflage plywood board covering the hole concealed behind a bramble of brush.

Nora scrambled out and made her way through the trees, doing her best not to rustle the fallen carpet of leaves or snap any twigs on the ground. She heard the men talking in hushed voices not too far away, moving stealthily through the forest.

She veered down into a shallow ravine, which at one time was a running stream and was now dried up. She followed the ditch to a small clearing where Lennie often frequented whenever he wanted to spend time by himself in the woods.

The massive creature was nowhere to be seen.

"Lennie, where are you?" Nora muttered.

A man came out of the trees. As soon as he saw Nora, he raised the barrel of his rifle and pointed the muzzle at her.

"Whoa," Nora said, thinking she might bluff him and gave the man a stern look. "You can't hunt here. This is private property."

"Where is it?" The man took a menacing step toward Nora.

"I don't know what you're talking about."

"Sure, you do. I know who you are, Professor Howard."

"I still don't know what you want."

"Where's that damn ape-thing of yours?"

"You better leave," Nora warned.

"How about I jog your memory." This time the man strode directly towards Nora. He flipped his rifle around with the butt stock out, ready to strike Nora across the face.

A dark shadow loomed over the man. Before he could turn around and see what it was, a giant hairy hand grabbed him by the arm and flung him twenty feet across the clearing into the trunk of a tree, snapping his spine.

The twelve-foot tall Yeren shook his fist ready for a fight and huffed at the dead man lying at the base of the tree.

Nora looked up and whispered, "Lennie, we have to get out of here."

Two men suddenly appeared; one with a tranquilizer gun, the other carrying a long pole with a looped wire cord on the end.

"Lennie, look out," Nora shouted.

Before the man could take aim, Lennie knocked the dart gun from his hands and backhanded him once with a powerful blow, cracking his sternum, and knocking the wind out of him. The man clutched his chest, wheezing, and fell to his knees.

The man with the pole tried to set the noose around Lennie's neck.

Lennie batted the pole way. He snatched the man off his feet with both hands, hoisted him up over his head, and then slammed the man to the ground, killing him instantly.

More men came out of the trees.

"Lennie, run!" Nora screamed. She darted into the brush and Lennie lumbered after her. She heard the men yelling and shots fired in the air that Nora knew were meant to scare her into stopping and giving up.

There was no way she would surrender Lennie to these men.

She kept running, hurtling over fallen branches, and dodging boulders. She glanced over her shoulder to make sure Lennie was still behind her.

That's when she sailed out over the edge of an embankment and went tumbling down a hill. She rolled down the rough terrain getting battered by stones jutting out of the ground and bushes.

Landing at the bottom, her body badly bruised, she felt like she had been tossed about in a cement mixer filled with rocks.

She couldn't move and had no idea of the extent of her injuries.

All she could do was lay helpless. Lennie roared from up above at his capturers while they surrounded him.

Nora gazed up the hillside and got a glimpse of Lennie spinning around in a circle, swinging his arms.

A body rolled down the rugged slope and landed a couple feet away from Nora.

Lying next to her, the man stared at her with glazed eyes. His head had been twisted backwards. Nora couldn't tell if the injury was from the fall or if Lennie had snapped his neck.

She heard a short burst of gunfire on the ridge.

Lennie let out a yowl that echoed in the lower canyon.

Blackness set in and Nora passed out.

39

A NO-SHOW

"Move out of our way," Mack shouted, shoving past a man holding a banner and knocking him into the crowd.

"Hey, watch it!" the man responded.

Mack ignored the protester and glanced over his shoulder. He could still see the black plumes of smoke from the train burning underground in the subway tunnel, venting up through the sidewalk grates a block away.

He glanced at the Metro worker in the orange safety vest, running behind him. "How much farther?"

"Next street down. We're almost there."

A throng of protestors had taken over the streets, impeding traffic, and barricading themselves in front of businesses so customers couldn't get inside, causing havoc so everything would screech to a standstill.

Generally, Mack was sympathetic to some of their causes but not today. A big man stood in his path. Mack elbowed him out of the way to make room for the Metro worker on his heels.

"That's it there!" the Metro worker shouted.

Mack ran up to the grate in the sidewalk and dropped to his knees so he could see through the bars.

Anna's panicked face looked up at him. "Mack, thank God," Anna cried out, waving her cell phone. "Get us out of here! Hurry!"

The Metro worker knelt and unlocked the padlock securing the grate. He used a special tool to dislodge the grill and lifted it off onto the cement sidewalk.

Anna clambered out of the hole, followed by Nick and Meg Wells. They scrambled away from the access hole.

"Is that all?" Mack asked. "No one else?"

In answer to his question, a giant death worm stretched six feet out of the hole. It contorted its body in an L-shape, its black head jerking from one side to the other, overwhelmed by all the different sounds coming at it in all directions.

Mack whipped his Glock out of the holster and fired three shots into the hideous worm. The 9-millimeter slugs punched through the creature like it was made of gelatin and splattered much of it against a brick wall. The vivisected worm slumped onto the cement and slipped back down into the subway access shaft.

The Metro worker scurried over and slid the heavy cover over the hole.

Mack stared at Anna who always dressed immaculately. His partner's impeccable black pantsuit was ruined, gray with soot, the jacket torn at the shoulder, her white shirt grimed, pants ripped at the knees, the leather on her shoes scratched and scuffed. Her face was smudged and her sleek, raven hair now a bird nest covered in dust. "Jeez, Anna, I don't think I've ever seen you look more radiant."

"Bug off, Hunter. Where the hell are we?"

Mack turned and glanced down the street. He could see the shrubbery near the entrance columns of the Longworth House Office Building where the senate hearing was most likely already in session. He glanced at Nick Wells. "Come on. We might just make it."

"But look at us," Nick said. He had dried blood on his face and his clothes were tattered and smirched. He looked like a survivor that had been shipwrecked on a deserted island.

Meg Wells's outfit looked like she had crawled out from the grave. "Nick's right, we can't go in there looking like this."

Mack put up his hand. "Sure we can. Hey, aren't you going in there to convince these senators that passing this crazy bill to protect these damn cryptids is a bad idea?"

"Well, yeah," Nick said.

"What do you think they're going to say when they see you in this condition and you tell them what happened on your way over. This is perfect."

"You're right."

"We better hurry," Anna said.

They raced down the street past the streetlamps perched on square concrete slabs and the long row of steel bollards for protecting the front of the government building from vehicle attacks.

Mack led the way up the granite steps and was the first one inside. He flashed his FBI credentials at the sheriff deputies posted at the metal detector as Anna, Nick, and Meg scrambled through the doorway.

"Sorry, folks, but we can't let you in," a deputy said.

"I know the hearing must already be in session but we really need to get in there," Anna said and then turned to Nick. "This man's testimony is crucial."

"Well, he'll have to come back tomorrow. The hearing's been postponed."

"But why?" Mack asked.

"Committee Chairman Senator Rollins is unable to conduct the hearing."

"I don't understand, he's the one that subpoenaed me," Nick said. "He has no idea what we had to go through to get here. Where can we find him?"

"That I can't tell you. He never showed up."

40

BAD KARMA

FBI Special Agent Mark Jennings couldn't believe his run of bad luck that plagued him throughout the early part of the day.

First, he had woken up late as the power had gone out in his place. Groping about in the dark and still groggy from the sleeping pill he had taken before turning in, he found his cell phone on the nightstand hoping to use it as a flashlight only to find the battery was dead, which was strange as he had put it on the charger before going to bed.

He ended up using the Maglite he always kept on the dresser top next to his service weapon and FBI shield so he could see in the bathroom while he took a quick shower and went back into the bedroom to get dressed.

When he left his apartment, he was surprised to see the lights on in the hallway.

The second thing to go wrong was when he went down to the underground garage and got into his government-issue sedan, pushed the start button and the car wouldn't start.

Reaching into the inside pocket of his suit jacket where he always kept the automobile's key fob, he realized it wasn't there. If there was one thing he never did, it was break a regimented discipline.

He figured the electronic key might have fallen out of his pocket while he was getting dressed in the dark so he went back up to his apartment and searched for the fob.

A half hour wasted, as it was nowhere to be found.

The third thing to further screw up his day was when he decided to use the apartment phone to call the Bureau to send along a car.

He wasn't a bit surprised to find the line was dead.

He knew he didn't have much time before he was expected to pick up Senator Jonathan Rollins from his lavish townhouse apartment and drive the committee chairman to oversee his government hearing.

He went to his nightstand, opened the drawer, took out his car keys to his Lexus and went down to the garage where it was parked on a separate level.

The fourth major thing to go wrong was discovering his car had been stolen.

That's when he realized no one could have this much bad karma.

By then, daylight was filtering through the sliding glass door leading out to the balcony. He conducted a thorough search and discovered someone had indeed broken in creating scratch marks when they jimmied the lock on his apartment door.

After taking off the back plate on his cell phone he instantly discovered why it wasn't working—the battery had been removed.

He pulled the credenza away from the wall where he kept the house phone on the dock and saw the telephone cord snipped.

By then he was getting a little paranoid knowing if someone was bold enough to sneak into his apartment and mess with his stuff, there was no telling what else they might have done.

He went into the bottom drawer of his nightstand, took out an electronic scanner, and began a sweep for laser beams and microwave transmission setups to see if there were any hidden cameras and audio bug listening devices.

He found no such devices after scanning the kitchen and dining room then the living room, bedroom, and finally his office.

On a lark, he went into his bedroom closet and opened the electrical control panel.

The main breaker had been turned off. He kicked himself for not checking it sooner. It meant that a prowler had been inside his bedroom while he had been sound asleep which made the situation even more unsettling. Had someone tampered with his sleeping pills?

His only alternative was to go down to the street and hail a taxicab to the senator's townhouse. Once there, he could phone the Bureau and expedite a car to be sent over.

Before leaving, a thought crossed his mind.

He drew his Glock service weapon and ejected the clip. Someone had removed the bullets. There were no rounds in the extra magazine he kept in his jacket pocket.

He was definitely being set up for a bad fall if he were engaged in a gunfight.

Taking a moment, he grabbed a box of 9-millimeter cartridges out of the bottom drawer of his nightstand, reloaded his gun and his spare clip.

When he came out of the downstairs lobby of his apartment complex, he found the sidewalks swarming with protesters, some of them marching in the streets.

It took him five minutes to flag a cab and another twenty minutes to arrive at Senator Rollins's townhouse.

He checked his watch as he rode up the elevator. He was cutting it close but he was confident he would be able to arrange a car and get the senator to the meeting on time.

Jennings got out of the elevator, strode down the hall, and knocked on the door.

When no one answered after a short wait, he knocked again.

He could hear footsteps on the other side of the door.

The deadbolt threw back and the door opened slightly.

Eva, the Rollins's housekeeper stared through the crack. She appeared nervous and looked like she had been crying.

Jennings immediately suspected something was wrong when she didn't let him in.

He gazed over her head and tried to get a peek inside. He saw no one lurking in the foyer.

"Is the senator in?" he asked, hoping Eva might say something to alert him to what was going on.

"Senator Rollins not feeling well," Eva replied, her lips quivering.

"What's wrong with him?"

"He say he got sick on my tamale pie."

Even though Jennings knew Eva to be an excellent cook as he had eaten a few meals at the Rollins' while watching the family, he also knew the senator would not eat tamale pie as he didn't like cornbread, complaining it was too dry.

"Should I summon a doctor?" Jennings asked, stalling for more time.

"No, Senor Jennings, I don't think so."

"So where is he now?"

"Upstairs with Amy."

"And Mrs. Collins?"

"She in the kitchen."

Jennings signaled Eva by nudging his head to the left. She responded with a subtle nod. Someone was standing behind the door, holding her captive.

He motioned with his thumb for her to get out from behind the door. As soon as she sidestepped, Jennings pushed through the door and came around at the man banging up against the wall with a knife in his hand.

Jennings instantly knew the man was a Crypto member as he wore dark clothes with a hooded sweatshirt and a balaclava Bigfoot mask covering his nose and chin.

The man lunged with the knife. Jennings grabbed his assailant by the wrist with his left hand and clutched the inside of the man's elbow, stopping the forward thrust, gaining control of the attack. Jennings followed through with a ramrod headbutt to the man's shoulder, which caused the man enough pain to drop his weapon.

Jennings held onto the man's arm and swung him around, and while doing so, drove the heel of his shoe into the man's shin, snapping the fibula and dropping him to the floor. He silenced the man with a quick jab, pulverizing the cartilage in his nose to a bloody mush and another sonic punch to the temple when he rolled his head, rendering him unconscious.

"Are you okay?" Jennings whispered to Eva.

"Si," Eva replied.

"Do you know if anyone is hurt?"

Eva shook her head.

Jennings peeked around the corner at the main living area where the senator had staged his cocktail party. There was no one in the room. He could see another Crypto standing in the kitchen guarding Margo Rollins seated a few feet away in the breakfast nook.

"How many men?" he asked Eva.

"One in kitchen, two upstairs," the housekeeper replied.

"Do they have guns?"

"Si, I think so."

Jennings knew he would never get all the way across the stately room without being seen by the man in the kitchen. He looked down at the unconscious man on the floor and got an idea. He took off his jacket and hung it on the coat rack by the door.

Luckily, the man hadn't bled all over his clothes. Jennings unzipped the man's sweatshirt and pulled it off of him. The agent put on the garment, zipping it up. He removed the man's mask and put it on. He pulled the hood over his head. He figured he could pass for the Crypto as long as he kept behind Eva and no one could see that he was wearing slacks and dress shoes instead of jeans and sneakers.

Jennings looked at Eva. "Unbutton your blouse."

"What?"

"And muss up your hair."

"But why?"

"I want them to think we just had sex. It's the only way I can stay close to you when we go in."

Eva gave him a puzzled look but did as he said.

"Let's go." Jennings put his hand on Eva's shoulder and followed her slowly across the elegant room.

The man in the kitchen glanced their way for a second and then stared back at Mrs. Rollins. He was dressed the same as the man Jennings had incapacitated and also wore a Bigfoot balaclava facemask, a common practice with the radical group, having factions that often shared the same cryptid identities.

As they approached the kitchen, Jennings noticed the man bobbing his head slightly and realized he was listening to music on his earbuds, which explained why he hadn't heard Jennings pummeling the man at the door.

Jennings made sure to stay behind the island in the middle of the kitchen so he couldn't be seen from the waist down and give himself away. He looked over at Mrs. Rollins and waited until their eyes locked. He reached up and pulled down his mask for a split second to reveal his full face while the man had his back turned listening to his music.

Mrs. Rollins gave him a quick smile.

Jennings heard footsteps coming down the wide staircase.

It was another Crypto, dressed in the same fashion. He came off the bottom step and walked onto the granite floor. He took one look at the disheveled housekeeper, shook his head, and glared at Jennings. "What the hell is wrong with you? Can't you keep it in your pants for five seconds? Jesus!" The man walked along the opposite side of the island and came up behind the other Crypto, slapping him on the back. The startled man spun around as the other man ripped the earbuds out from under the hood of his sweatshirt.

"How many times do I have to tell you? Enough with the damn music!" He reached in the man's sweatshirt pocket and confiscated his iPhone. "Now do your job!"

Jennings could hear the tinny music coming out of the earbuds. He moved closer to Eva and whispered in her ear. "Ask if they're hungry."

"Mrs. Rollins," Eva said. "It is almost time for you to eat."

The Crypto seemingly in charge glared at the housekeeper. "Seriously? You're worried about food?"

"I'm diabetic," Mrs. Rollins said. "It's important I keep my blood sugar up."

"Well, if that's the case, let's all eat." The Crypto waved to Eva to start preparing some food.

Eva reached up and removed a large skillet hanging with other pots and pans over the kitchen island. She placed the frying pan on a wooden cutting board.

She went over to the double-door refrigerator recessed in the wall. She opened one side, took out a carton of eggs, a half-gallon jug of milk, and a package of shredded cheese and put them on the counter. She took out a plastic bag of mushrooms and a white onion, closed the refrigerator and brought the items over to the cutting board. She reached down, opened a cupboard door, and took out a mixing bowl.

Eva grabbed a carving knife from the block.

"Careful there," the Crypto warned.

The housekeeper gave the man a meek nod. She put a few mushrooms on the cutting board and began slicing them.

Jennings had been distracted watching Eva that he hadn't noticed the Crypto in charge step around the island. "What the hell?" he shouted when he noticed the agent's suit trousers and shined shoes.

The man lunged and grabbed Jennings by the throat with both hands. Before he could apply pressure, Jennings grabbed a wrist with his left hand, shot up his right arm, and crossed over, pinning his attacker's arms against his side. He used the momentum and slammed the man's lower back into a granite bull nose corner of the island.

Jennings released the man and stepped back. The man stumbled toward him in excruciating pain. The agent delivered a powerful left hook into the man's right side below his ribcage, striking him in the liver and doubling him over. The man's skull cracked like an eggshell on the hard tile when he hit the floor.

The other Crypto stepped around the other side of the island.

Right into a mean swing of the skillet, which fractured his forehead and sent him sprawling on his back.

"Ever think of trying out for the Nationals?" Jennings joked, watching Eva toss the large frying pan on the cutting board.

"No, but my son might."

"Let's hope it runs in the family."

Mrs. Rollins got up, went over, and hugged her housekeeper. "Thank you, Eva. You are so brave."

"It's my job."

"So you said there is one more?" Jennings asked.

"Yes," Mrs. Rollins said. "I believe he's with Jonathan and Amy in my husband's study upstairs."

Jennings took off the sweatshirt and removed the bandana facemask. He undid the top button of his dress shirt, loosened his tie, and drew his service weapon. "All right. Don't go outside or use the phone, not until I've neutralized the situation."

He went up the stairs to the hallway and followed it to the senator's study.

The door was open.

Senator Rollins and his daughter, Amy, were sitting on a long couch in the center of the room.

A Crypto stood at the end of the couch. He had his arms crossed over his chest and was holding a revolver.

When he saw Jennings at the threshold, he said, "Well, well, look who we have here. I'm surprised you made it. What did you do, walk?"

"So you're the one that was in my apartment," Jennings said.

"Did you know you snore?" the Crypto said, snorting behind his mask. "You're lucky I didn't slit your throat while you slept."

"Maybe you should have." Jennings raised his service weapon.

The Crypto laughed. "And maybe you should have checked your gun FBI man." He unfolded his arms and swung his gun muzzle at Senator Rollins.

Jennings de-escalated the situation by shooting the Crypto in the head.

41

EASY DOES IT

Abe strolled by the nurses's station and stopped at the last room down the hall. He looked in and saw Clare scooting off the edge of the hospital bed while a nurse held the handles on the wheelchair so it wouldn't slip out from under her.

A cast covered Clare's forearm and was in a sling. She had a yellowish brush on her right cheek. She moved gingerly as though any second something might break and she would go toppling to the floor.

Once Clare was safely in the wheelchair, the nurse said, "I'll be right back with your meds and then you can go."

"Thanks," Clare said.

Abe stepped aside so the nurse could pass through the door. He went into the room and sat on the edge of the bed next to Clare as they waited for the nurse to return.

"How's the arm?" he asked.

"Not too bad. It's my shoulder that's killing me. And my three cracked ribs. Not to mention my face. I feel like a wet sack of shit, excuse my French."

"Sounds terrible. I'm sure you'll be feeling better once you're home and pumped up with those lovely pain pills," Abe said, hoping to lighten the mood, knowing that his wife was a strong woman and if she was complaining of pain then it was extreme.

"You know, I noticed when that damn bird took me over the house that you might want to get on the roof and replace some of those shingles."

"Is that right?" Abe replied. "Just be thankful that damn bird broke your fall or we wouldn't be having this conversation."

"Consider it something to put on your to-do list."

"I'll keep that under advisement."

"You do that. Any word on the funerals?"

"They're scheduled for next week," Abe said, knowing there were plans to give deputies Kurtz and Dobson a ceremonious burial with a special honor guard and there would be law enforcement personnel attending from agencies in four counties.

Clare grimaced as a new pain kicked up. "What's keeping the nurse?"

"I'm right here," the nurse said, overhearing Clare from the hall. She handed Clare a white paper bag stuffed with medications.

Abe got behind the wheelchair and grabbed the handles. "I'll take the reins from here."

"Sure thing, Sheriff," the nurse said. "You take good care of her. Bye Clare."

"Bye, and thank you."

Abe wheeled Clare out of the room and down the hall to the elevator. He pushed Clare in and they rode down to the lobby.

Rounder was lying on the floor next to the front entrance door. As soon as he saw Clare, he got up and bounded across the room.

"Easy there," Abe said, afraid the 130-pound dog might leap into Clare's lap.

Instead, the massive canine came to a halt inches from crashing into Clare's slippers set on the footrests.

Clare kneaded Rounder's scruff. "Looks like someone missed me."

Rounder responded with a fierce, resonating bark that bounced off the walls.

"Sounds like he speaks for the both of us," Abe said with a grin.

Clare started to chuckle then winced. "Please, don't make me laugh."

"Come on, boy. Let's get this sourpuss home." Abe pushed Clare out through the automatic doors. Rounder trotted beside the wheelchair as they headed for the Bronco parked at the curb.

42

CONCERTO

Laney smiled at Harvey as he entered the rear of the greenhouse with his wife. "Please, if you'll put these on," Laney said and handed them each a hemp bracelet. They slipped the bands around their wrists.

"Thank you so much for inviting us," Harvey's wife said.

Harvey gave Laney a peck on the cheek like he would his own daughter. "Yeah, looks like I'll be sticking around for a little while longer, thanks to you and Allen."

"I'm so glad," Laney responded. "Toby will show you to your seats."

As Harvey and his wife were the last to arrive, Laney shut the door.

Laney had put her red hair in a tight braid and was wearing a flowery summer dress and sandals. She watched Toby usher the couple to two vacant seats of the 30 foldout chairs arranged in three rows of ten. Toby sat in the last empty chair next to Alice. Everyone faced the interior of the greenhouse and its splendorous foliage.

Allen stepped out from behind a seven-foot high heavenly bamboo and stood next to Laney. "Quite the turnout. Looks like everyone from the senior center is here." Allen was stylishly dressed for the occasion in his green kilt—and nothing else. The man-skirt was the perfect accessory with his emerald skin.

Laney walked over to the lectern, which was really only a potting table with tall legs, and gazed out at the audience. "Hello, everyone. So nice to see you."

Everyone smiled and returned the greeting.

"Before we begin, Allen and I would like to apologize."

"Apologize for what?" an elderly woman blurted. "Most of us wouldn't be here if it wasn't for you and your husband."

"I know," Laney said. "It's just that we were hoping to permanently rid you of all your ailments, which is why we can no longer call our plants a cure-all, especially after so many of you have relapsed after being in remission. I'm afraid our medicinal herbs that were stolen and we got back are only a short-term solution. That is why we are now calling them longevity plants.

"You have to believe me when I say Allen will not rest until he has discovered the ultimate cure for all your diseases."

"Hey, sure we want to be around for our loved ones," Toby spoke up, holding hands with Alice, "but I really don't think any of us want to live forever."

"We'd bankrupt the Social Security System," a man said.

Everyone had a good laugh.

"Hell, our kids would be pushing us down the stairs so they could get their inheritances."

Laney smiled at the tightly knit group of seniors sharing a bit of humor, as it was the best way to cope with life. "I'm so glad you all feel that way."

"I was wondering," said the same man that had made everyone laugh, "what is up with these bracelets?"

"You might say they're to enhance your experience for this evening," Laney said, not wanting to scare everyone by telling them if they weren't wearing the hemp bracelets, they would be in mortal danger from the man-eating plants in the nearby flowerbeds.

But there was another reason.

"Take a whiff of your bracelets." Laney held the hemp to her nose and inhaled deeply.

Everyone followed suit.

"Smells musty," Alice said, twitching her nose.

"Makes my nostrils itch," said the woman sitting beside her.

Hearing the comments, Laney said, "That's because Allen dusted the hemp with a little psychedelic mushroom powder."

"He did what?" a woman gasped.

"Not to be alarmed," Laney assured everyone. "It's quite harmless and will wear off before the evening's over."

Allen joined Laney at the makeshift podium. He put his arm around his wife and stared out over the audience. "And now everyone, please sit back and enjoy the performance."

Laney went to a control panel and dimmed the lights in the greenhouse.

Blue phosphorescent lichen illuminated the interior of the greenhouse.

Symphonic music began to play on the speakers, violins setting the mood, each section of the orchestra progressively joining in.

Laney watched the audience and could see their eyes brightening and their mouths forming into silly smiles. The quick-acting shrooms had kicked in. Feeling dreamy herself, Laney sat on the edge of a planter box and stared out at the foliage undulating to the rhythm of the music.

Allen stepped barefoot between the planter boxes, waving his arms in the air like a conductor in front of a symphony orchestra. Each time he reacted to the music, the plants around him would mimic his every movement.

The blue lichen illuminating the greenhouse changed rapidly to blue-green and back again repeatedly, giving the illusion of a flickering strobe light.

Everyone began to rock gently in their seats, keeping tempo with the swaying plants; a sea of blossoming flowers opening and closing to each beat of the music.

The two giant man-eating trees at the far end of the greenhouse raised their arm-like boughs and opened their finger-like branches, casting eerie shadow puppets on the glass pane windows.

Allen was dancing and twirling euphorically; his epidermis from head to toe a rainbow pointillism collage of tiny dots.

Laney knew she was tripping when Allen's plants drew their bow-like leaves across their stalks to accompany the symphonic string section performing over the speakers and the gable-shaped structure filled with the melodious sound of a thousand violas.

43

A SMALL WORLD

Nick parked the rental car in the lot reserved for visitors and shut off the engine.

Meg stared at the campus map in the brochure on her lap. She looked up and pointed to a shale walkway cutting through a large area of freshly mowed lawn. "I think Gabe's dormitory is that way."

"Didn't he say he'd meet us outside the Student Union?"

"You're right. That's near the cafeteria."

Nick climbed out of the car. He waited for Meg to get out and close her door before hitting the button on the driver-side armrest and locking all the doors before closing his. "How did he sound to you over the phone when you told him we were dropping by for a visit?"

"A little surprised. I think we caught him off guard."

"Well, we'll cut him some slack and skip his dorm room," Nick said.

"He'll appreciate that," Meg said. "I'm so glad to be out of D.C. Nice to have that all behind us."

"Think I convinced them?"

"If that bill passes, there's something seriously wrong with this government."

They headed down a walkway toward a building that looked like it had been built in the late 1800s; the stone façade covered with ivy.

Before reaching the granite steps leading up to the columned entrance, Nick and Meg stopped when they heard a booming voice.

A young woman holding a bullhorn stood on the pedestal at the base of a bronze statue of a horse reared up on its hind legs with a cavalryman pulling back on the reins. A crowd of about fifty students had stopped between classes to listen.

"It's time to stand up to the rich and stop big business such as Wilde Enterprises from destroying our planet," the impassioned student shouted. "Before it is too late! Global warming is real! Climate change is real! Forget all those ignorant politicians that say differently! We must stop needless deforestation and illegal logging especially in the Amazon rainforest. We must protect the environment at all costs!

"Just like we need to say NO to fossil fuels! Fining big corporations with emissions taxes doesn't resolve the problem! Stopping the polluters DOES! Shut the refineries down! Stop the polluting! Shut 'em down! Save our planet! Shut 'em down!"

A few of the students watching her speak began to chant, "Shut 'em down! Shut 'em down!"

Nick hooked his arm in Meg's and they walked off.

"Nice to see young people getting involved," Meg said.

Nick spotted their son standing by the entrance to another building. "That must be the cafeteria."

They walked over and greeted their son, Meg hugging her boy, Nick giving Gabe a firm handshake before embracing him with a pat on the back.

"If I knew you were coming I would have baked a cake," Gabe quipped.

"That's something your mom would say," Nick said. "Since when do you bake?" "So how are your classes?" Meg asked.

"Good, all good."

"Girlfriend?"

"As a matter of fact, yes."

"Will we be meeting her?" Meg asked.

"Of course. Here she comes."

Nick and Meg turned and saw the same young woman that had been protesting with the bullhorn. She walked up to Gabe and gave him a kiss on the cheek.

"Mom, Dad, I'd like you to meet Caroline Rollins."

"You wouldn't by any chance be related to Senator Jonathan Rollins?" Meg asked.

"Why, yes. He's my father."

"Well, isn't this a small world," Nick said.

44

HEAD OF THE SNAKE

Mack and Anna slipped on their bulletproof vests while agents Al Johnson, Dirk Brown, Tony Murdock, and Jason Patterson stood by armed with combat shotguns and assault rifles, everyone identified with the bold yellow FBI lettering on the back of their blue jackets.

The team was congregated in a side alley between an abandoned brownstone tenement and an old meat packing plant where they were preparing a surprise raid.

"Is it true Jennings took out four of them at the senator's home?" Johnson asked.

"Three," Mack replied. "One in the hospital was coldcocked by the housekeeper."

"Good for her."

"So how many do you think are inside?" asked Brown.

"From what Jennings could gather from the suspect, maybe a dozen."

"Along with the head honcho we hope," Anna added.

"That's right," Mack said. "Time to cut the head off the snake. You all know what to do. Be careful in there. Let's move out."

Mack led the way turning the corner and headed for the loading dock. Anna stayed close behind, the other agents following single file.

As the buildings were located in a section of town awaiting City Hall's approval for demolition, the area was deserted.

Mack approached a door next to a closed aluminum roll-up.

The doorknob had been punched out.

"Tell Johnson to ditch the battering ram," Mack told Anna. She whispered to Brown behind her who passed it on. Mack heard some muttering and the heavy ram clunk on the cement.

Mack pushed open the door.

The open space inside the gloomy warehouse was cluttered with rusted three-rack pushcarts and long brown-stained metal tables, a defunct staging area for shipping the packaged meat.

Mack looked to his right and saw the cavernous structure sectioned off with a wall divider that stretched halfway to the rafters. Straight ahead, metal stairs led up to a catwalk and an office. To the left, a plastic strip curtain hung over an entry obscuring the other side.

Mack gave the signal.

Murdock and Patterson sprinted to the right.

Mack and Anna rushed toward the plastic curtain while Johnson and Brown dashed for the steel staircase.

Two Cryptos burst out of the office with automatic weapons and fired down at the two agents out in the open. Brown took multiple hits to the head and chest. Johnson managed to take out one of his assailants even though his legs had been cut out from under him.

Mack knew the agents were dead. He put the man on the catwalk in his sights and fired off a quick burst from his Glock. The gunner's weapon slipped from his fingers and he fell over the railing, landing face down on the cement floor with a bone-cracking splat.

Murdock and Patterson dropped to crouch positions. They panned the warehouse with their guns: Murdock with his assault rifle, Patterson ready for a close-up attack with his combat shotgun.

"Jesus, Mack," Anna said. "Did we walk into a trap?"

"Shit, looks that way."

Murdock was looking at Mack when four men charged out from their hiding place and opened fire. A wave of bullets ripped through the plastered walls.

Patterson blasted a man in the face with a load of buckshot. He pumped another cartridge into the chamber and knocked another one off his feet with a shot to the gut.

Murdock took a hit to the leg, still managing to drop the man who shot him.

The remaining Crypto turned to run.

Patterson nailed the fleeing man in the back.

He rushed over to Murdock. "How bad?" he asked then saw the ragged wound in the agent's thigh. "We're getting you out of here."

"Go with Hunter and Rivers," Murdock said.

"You sure?"

"Yeah," Murdock replied, drawing his service weapon. "Use my belt."

Patterson unbuckled Murdock's belt around his waist and slipped it out of the pant loops. He fastened the leather strap around the upper part of Murdock's thigh near his groin and cinched it tight. "That should hold you."

Murdock winced. "Thanks."

"Do me a favor," Patterson said.

"What's that?"

"Don't die before we get back."

"I'll do my best," Murdock groaned.

Patterson ran over to Mack and Anna.

"How's he doing?" Mack asked.

"Hanging in there."

Mack pushed through the hanging strips.

Holding his pistol in a two-handed grip, he stared down the barrel at a narrow passageway. He started down the corridor, stopping when he saw an adjacent room with meat hooks dangling from the ceiling.

"Mack, look out!" Anna yelled when a Crypto popped out from around a corner with a machine gun and strafed the hallway with a deadly barrage of bullets.

Mack and Anna dove into the adjacent room.

Patterson was cut down and hit the floor.

"Through there," Mack said, spotting another doorway.

Mack and Anna crashed through the meat hooks causing them to clang into one another. They ran through the doorway and found themselves in a large room, which looked to be the Cryptos's main hideout.

Two men jumped up from behind their laptops and grabbed for their guns on the table.

Anna charged into the room shooting them both while Mack blasted another one standing by a number of wooden crates stacked against the wall.

Mack heard the meat hooks banging together and heavy footsteps rushing toward the doorway. He flattened himself against the wall, and when the man with the machine gun stepped over the threshold, Mack shot him point blank in the temple.

Both agents braced themselves for another attack, aiming their weapons at the doorway. After a few seconds, Mack said, "What do you think?"

"Sounds quiet."

"Better check Patterson."

Anna slipped out of the room. She returned thirty seconds later shaking her head.

"Shit." Mack went to the crates and removed a lid. "Whoa, take a look at this."

Anna came over and stared down at the freshly oiled gun parts partially wrapped in wax paper as a rust preventative.

Mack popped the lid on another container and found it loaded with assembled AK-47s. He looked at the other crates. "There must be enough guns here to start a small revolution."

Anna pushed a dead man off the table. She sat in a chair to examine the data on one of the laptops while Mack went around, unmasking the dead men.

After he had seen every man's face, he said, "They're so young. I doubt any of them could be the leader."

"I may have found something," Anna said.

Mack stepped behind his partner and looked over her shoulder at the gun manufacturer website page on the screen. "Is this where they got the guns?"

"Looks like it. This company is a division of Wilde Enterprises. I think we just discovered who is funding the Cryptos."

"So our snake is Carter Wilde," Mack said.

"Looks like our rattler has suddenly become a python."

"Shit, Murdock!" Mack dashed out of the room and ran back to the main warehouse and found the agent trying to stand up. "Easy there," Mack said, draping Murdock's arm over his shoulder so the man wouldn't fall.

"Where's Patterson?" Murdock asked.

"He didn't make it."

"Shit!"

Anna came in with her cell phone pressed to her ear. She ended the call and looked at Mack. "They're on their way."

"Good," Mack said. "Let's get out of here."

Anna supported Murdock on the other side and the three went outside to wait in the sunshine away from the carnage.

45

THE BIG LUG

Jack sat across from Miguel at his friend's kitchen table cluttered with empty Modelo beer cans, shot glasses, and a bottle of Cazul 100 agave tequila. Miguel tipped the Cazul and refilled their shot glasses. "To one hell of a shitty day," he toasted.

"I'll second that," Jack slurred and downed the shooter in one gulp.

Maria came into the kitchen. "Will you two keep it down?"

Miguel looked up at his wife and put his fingers to his lips. "Shhh."

"Don't be a jerk."

"Sorry."

"You guys shouldn't have gotten her drinking, especially with the medication she's taking," Maria scolded the two men.

"Is she okay?" Jack asked.

"She's lying down on our bed. Poor thing cried herself to sleep."

"Can't believe those bastards left her in the woods," Jack said.

"I think she's more devastated not knowing what happened to Lenny than worrying about herself," Maria said.

Jack leaned on the table and looked up at Maria. "Might as well come join us."

"What the hell." Maria pulled up a chair.

Miguel poured her a shot of tequila.

Maria gulped it right down.

Miguel looked over at the kitchen door and grinned. "Remember when Lenny ripped off our door?"

"Oh, yeah," Jack said, recalling the barbeque the Wallas held for a few close friends. Lenny had caught the scent of the Bigfoot that had previously broken into the Walla's home and had mistakenly thought the creature was on the other side of the door and tore it off the hinges. "Did I ever tell you about his first swimming lesson?"

"Is that when he fell in the pool at that skyrise?" Maria asked.

"Hard for a twelve-foot Yeren to drown in ten feet of water," Jack said.

"That's Lenny for you," Miguel said. He poured more tequila in their shot glasses. "I miss the big lug," Jack said, feeling melancholy.

"Any idea where they might have taken him?" Maria asked.

"Not really. Before I begin searching for Lenny, I have to be sure Nora's going to be okay."

"Jack, she'll never by okay, not until you find Lenny."

"Hell Maria, he could be anywhere," Miguel said.

"Then you two better start looking."

46

BON VOYAGE

Lyle Mason leaned on the railing, enjoying the cold air on his face while he took in the spectacular view of the sapphire blue ocean from the observation deck outside the ship's bridge five stories up from the main deck. Three days at sea and his stomach was still queasy but the Dramamine pills were beginning to calm the effects of the seasickness. At least he wasn't spending most of the day when they first left port, doubled over in his cabin, puking his guts.

It was especially nice to have a reprieve from the overbearing smells of the livestock on board. He had heard the massive cargo vessel was carrying more than 14,000 sheep, 3,000 head of cattle, and of course, the creatures not listed on the ship's manifest.

Not wanting to be gone for too long, Mason turned and walked by the series of windows facing out from the ship's bridge. He rounded the corner and took the steel stairwell down to the next level. Rows upon rows of noisy ventilation turbines sucked out the ammonia and toxic odors from the stockades below, expelling the foul air out the exhaust stacks topside even though the pen areas were on open decks with railing walls.

Mason continued down into the belly of the ship. It was like navigating Noah's Ark hearing the cacophony of bellowing and bleating animals. He kept descending until he reached the internal level below the main deck. A narrow passageway took him to a sealed hatch. He turned the wheel and stepped through into a massive area half the size of a football field with twenty or more enclosed stockades.

The creatures down here sounded much different from those on the upper levels.

A man with red hair, wearing overalls, stood in front of a control panel. He looked up and saw Mason approaching. "Ah, good. You're back."

"Something wrong?" Mason asked.

"I can't seem to get the mixture right for the Xing-Xings. Damn things won't calm down. I'm afraid if I increase their dosage I might kill them," Todd Ramsey said.

"Yeah, we wouldn't want that." Mason looked at the computer readouts that showed the sedation levels administered to the drinking water in each pen. "You're right. Any more and it might kill them. I'm sure they'll wear themselves out soon enough and fall asleep."

The six young Xing-Xings were dashing about their enclosure like a bunch of lunatics, screeching at the top of their lungs. It was enough to make anyone go mad. Even though the golden-faced baboons weren't particularly big, Mason knew each fifty-pound primate was incredibly strong and weren't to be trifled with.

"Need a break?" Mason asked.

"Nah. Let's just ignore them." Ramsey started down the wide aisle between the other stockades.

Mason walked alongside him.

"How's the arm?" Ramsey asked.

"Functional." Since the vicious tiger attack and after forty-five stitches to sew his arm back together, Mason was experiencing bouts of shooting pain, having trouble flexing his left hand and his fingers would go numb. He raised his arm up so Ramsey could get a good look at the patchwork that looked like an ill-conceived quilt.

"Damn, Mason. That thing did a number on you."

"You ain't kidding."

They stopped and looked in at the dozen *Caudipeteryx*, the turkey-sized dinosaurs milled together in the middle of their enclosure like conspirators planning an escape.

"How's the new one?" Ramsey asked as they strolled over to the next caged-in area.

"Not too happy, I'm afraid," Mason replied.

"Can you blame him?"

"Not really."

Mason and Ramsey peered through the bars at the giant creature sitting despondently on the cold deck.

"I've heard this one is the most revered in the Chinese culture."

"That's what they say," Mason said. He pounded on the bars to get the creature's attention. "Did you hear that Lenny? Soon you're going to be quite the celebrity."

TO THE READER

I hope you enjoyed *CRYPTID NATION*. You can learn more about Allen Moss and his wife, Laney, and how Jack Tremens and Miguel Walla became cryptid hunters in *CRYPTID ISLAND*, the exciting prequel to *CRYPTID ZOO*. Please join them as they continue their adventures in *CRYPTID COUNTRY, CRYPTID CIRCUS, CRYPTID NATION* and coming soon by Severed Press *CRYPTID KINGDOM.*

ACKNOWLEDGEMENTS

I would like to thank Gary Lucas, Nichola Meaburn, Romana Baotic, and all the wonderful people working with Severed Press that helped with this book. It's truly amazing how folks we may never meet and who live in the most incredible places in the world can truly enrich our lives. A special thanks to my wonderful daughter and faithful beta reader, Genene Griffiths Ortiz for her enthusiasm and making this so much fun. And of course, I would like to thank you, the reader, for taking the time to share these bizarre and incredible journeys with me.

ABOUT THE AUTHOR

Gerry Griffiths lives in San Jose, California, with his family and their four rescue dogs and a cat. He is a Horror Writers Association member and has over thirty published short stories in various anthologies and magazines, along with a collection entitled *Creatures*. He is also the author of *Silurid, The Beasts of Stoneclad Mountain, Death Crawlers, Deep in the Jungle, The Next World, Battleground Earth, Down From Beast Mountain, Terror Mountain, Cryptid Zoo, Cryptid Country, Cryptid Island, Cryptid Circus*, and *Cryptid Nation*.

CHECK OUT OTHER GREAT CRYPTID NOVELS

BIGFOOT WAR
by Eric S. Brown

Now a feature film from Origin Releasing. For the first time ever, all three core books of the Bigfoot War series have been collected into a single tome of Sasquatch Apocalypse horror. Remastered and reedited this book chronicles the original war between man and beast from the initial battles in Babblecreek through the apocalypse to the wastelands of a dark future world where Sasquatch reigns supreme and mankind struggles to survive. If you think you've experienced Bigfoot Horror before, think again. Bigfoot War sets the bar for the genre and will leave you praying that you never have to go into the woods again.

CRYPTID ZOO
by Gerry Griffiths

As a child, rare and unusual animals, especially cryptid creatures, always fascinated Carter Wilde.

Now that he's an eccentric billionaire and runs the largest conglomerate of high-tech companies all over the world, he can finally achieve his wildest dream of building the most incredible theme park ever conceived on the planet...CRYPTID ZOO.

Even though there have been apparent problems with the project, Wilde still decides to send some of his marketing employees and their families on a forced vacation to assess the theme park in preparation for Opening Day.

Nick Wells and his family are some of those chosen and are about to embark on what will become the most terror-filled weekend of their lives—praying they survive.

STEP RIGHT UP AND GET YOUR FREE PASS...

TO CRYPTID ZOO

CHECK OUT OTHER GREAT CRYPTID NOVELS

SWAMP MONSTER MASSACRE
by **Hunter Shea**

The swamp belongs to them. Humans are only prey. Deep in the overgrown swamps of Florida, where humans rarely dare to enter, lives a race of creatures long thought to be only the stuff of legend. They walk upright but are stronger, taller and more brutal than any man. And when a small boat of tourists, held captive by a fleeing criminal, accidentally kills one of the swamp dwellers' young, the creatures are filled with a terrifyingly human emotion—a merciless lust for vengeance that will paint the trees red with blood.

TERROR MOUNTAIN
by **Gerry Griffiths**

When Marcus Pike inherits his grandfather's farm and moves his family out to the country, he has no idea there's an unholy terror running rampant about the mountainous farming community. Sheriff Avery Anderson has seen the heinous carnage and the mutilated bodies. He's also seen the giant footprints left in the snow—Bigfoot tracks. Meanwhile, Cole Wagner, and his wife, Kate, are prospecting their gold claim farther up the valley, unaware of the impending dangers lurking in the woods as an early winter storm sets in. Soon the snowy countryside will run red with blood on TERROR MOUNTAIN.

CHECK OUT OTHER GREAT BIGFOOT NOVELS

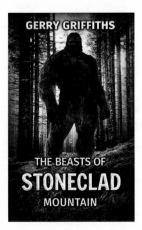

THE BEASTS OF STONECLAD MOUNTAIN
by **Gerry Griffiths**

Clay Morgan is overjoyed when he is offered a place to live in a remote wilderness at the base of a notorious mountain. Locals say there are Bigfoot living high up in the dense mountainous forest. Clay is skeptic at first and thinks it's nothing more than tall tales.

But soon Clay becomes a believer when giant creatures invade his new home and snatch his baby boy, Casey.

Now, Clay and his wife, Mia, must rescue their son with the help of Clay's uncle and his dog, a journey up the foreboding mountain that will take them into an unimaginable world...straight into hell!

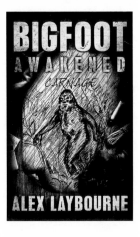

BIGFOOT AWAKENED
by **Alex Laybourne**

A weekend away with friends was supposed to be fun. One last chance for Jamie to blow off some steam before she leaves for college, but when the group make a wrong turn, fun is the last thing they find.

From the moment they pass through a small rural town they are being hunted by whatever abominations live in the woods.

Yet, as the beasts attack and the truth is revealed, they learn that despite everything, man still remains the most terrifying evil of them all.

Made in United States
North Haven, CT
10 December 2021

12193311R00098